Black BEAUTY

by Anna Sewell   retold by L. L. Owens   illustrated by Jennifer Tanner

Librarian Reviewer
Allyson A.W. Lyga MS
Library Media/Graphic Novel Consultant
Fulbright Memorial Fund Scholar, author

Reading Consultant
Mark DeYoung
Classroom Teacher, Edina Public Schools, MN
BA in Elementary Education, Central College
MS in Curriculum & Instruction, University of Minnesota

Graphic Revolve is published by Stone Arch Books,
151 Good Counsel Drive, P.O. Box 669,
Mankato, Minnesota 56002.
www.stonearchbooks.com

Library of Congress Cataloging-in-Publication Data
Owens, L. L.
    Black Beauty / by Anna Sewell; retold by L.L. Owens; illustrated by Jennifer
Tanner.
    p. cm.—(Graphic Revolve)
    ISBN-13: 978-1-59889-046-4 (hardcover)
    ISBN-10: 1-59889-046-8 (hardcover)
    ISBN-13: 978-1-59889-217-8 (paperback)
    ISBN-10: 1-59889-217-7 (paperback)
    1. Graphic novels. I. Tanner, Jennifer. II. Sewell, Anna, 1820–1878. Black
Beauty. III. Title. IV. Series.
PN6727.O985B63 2007
741.5'973—dc22   2006007691

Summary: Black Beauty grows up in the fields and horse meadows of Victorian
England. His peaceful childhood fades away as he faces human cruelty and
mistreatment in a world that cares little for the happiness of animals.

Credits
Art Director: Heather Kindseth
Graphic Designer: Kay Fraser

1 2 3 4 5 6 11 10 09 08 07 06

Printed in the United States of America.

Table of CONTENTS

INTRODUCING . . .

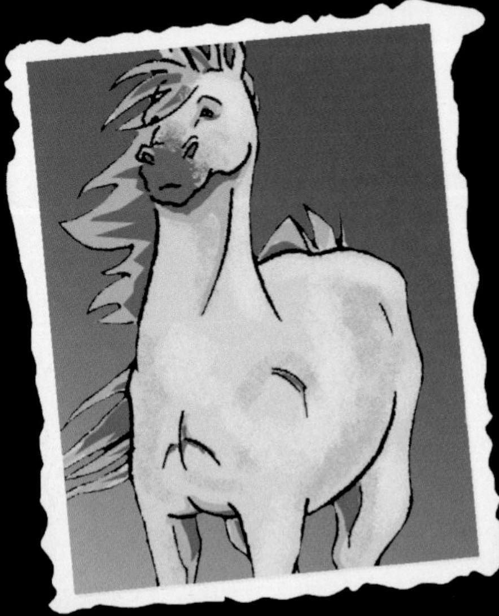

Duchess

Black Beauty's mother

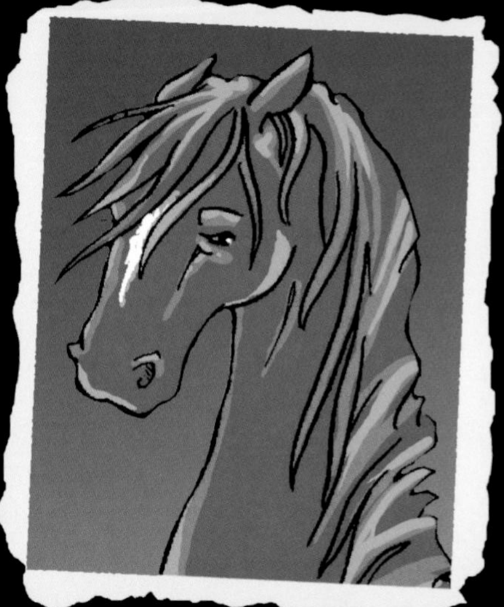

Ginger

Black Beauty's carriage partner and friend at Birtwick Park.

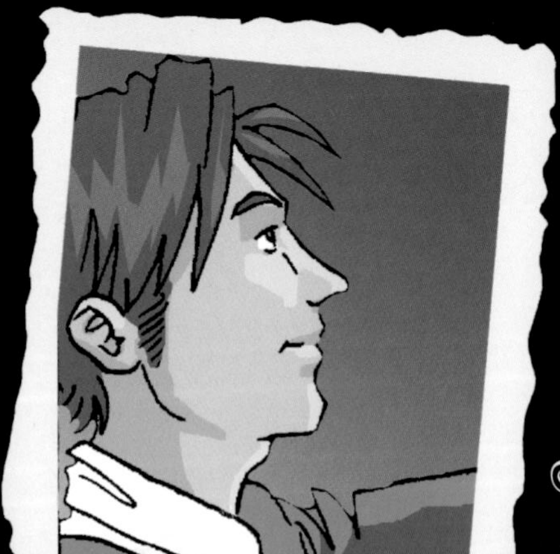

Jerry

A cabbie who owns Black Beauty

Black Beauty

Joe Green
A stable boy

Merrylegs
Black Beauty's stable mate
and friend at Birtwick Park.

Chapter 1 ★ My Early Home

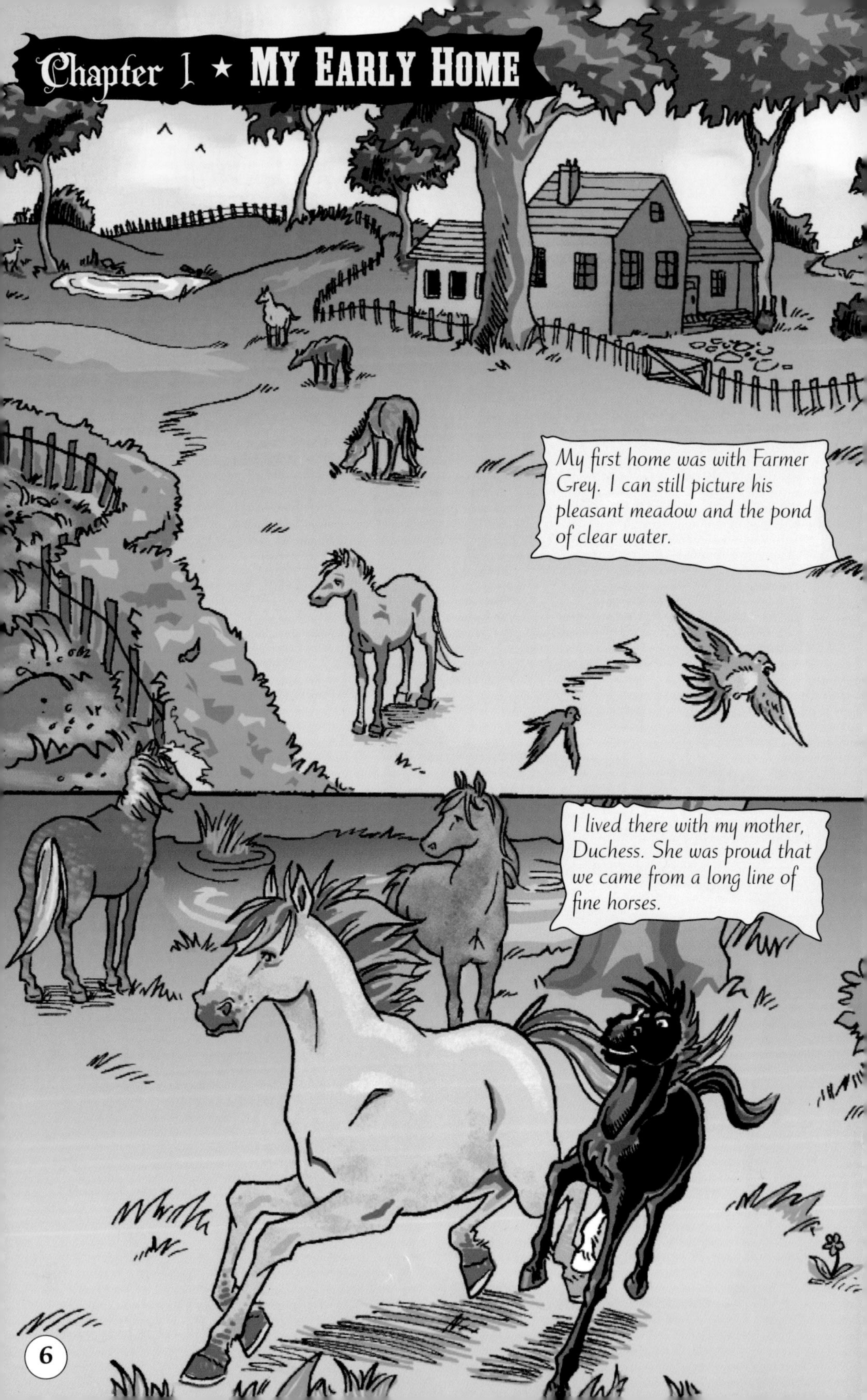
My first home was with Farmer Grey. I can still picture his pleasant meadow and the pond of clear water.
I lived there with my mother, Duchess. She was proud that we came from a long line of fine horses.

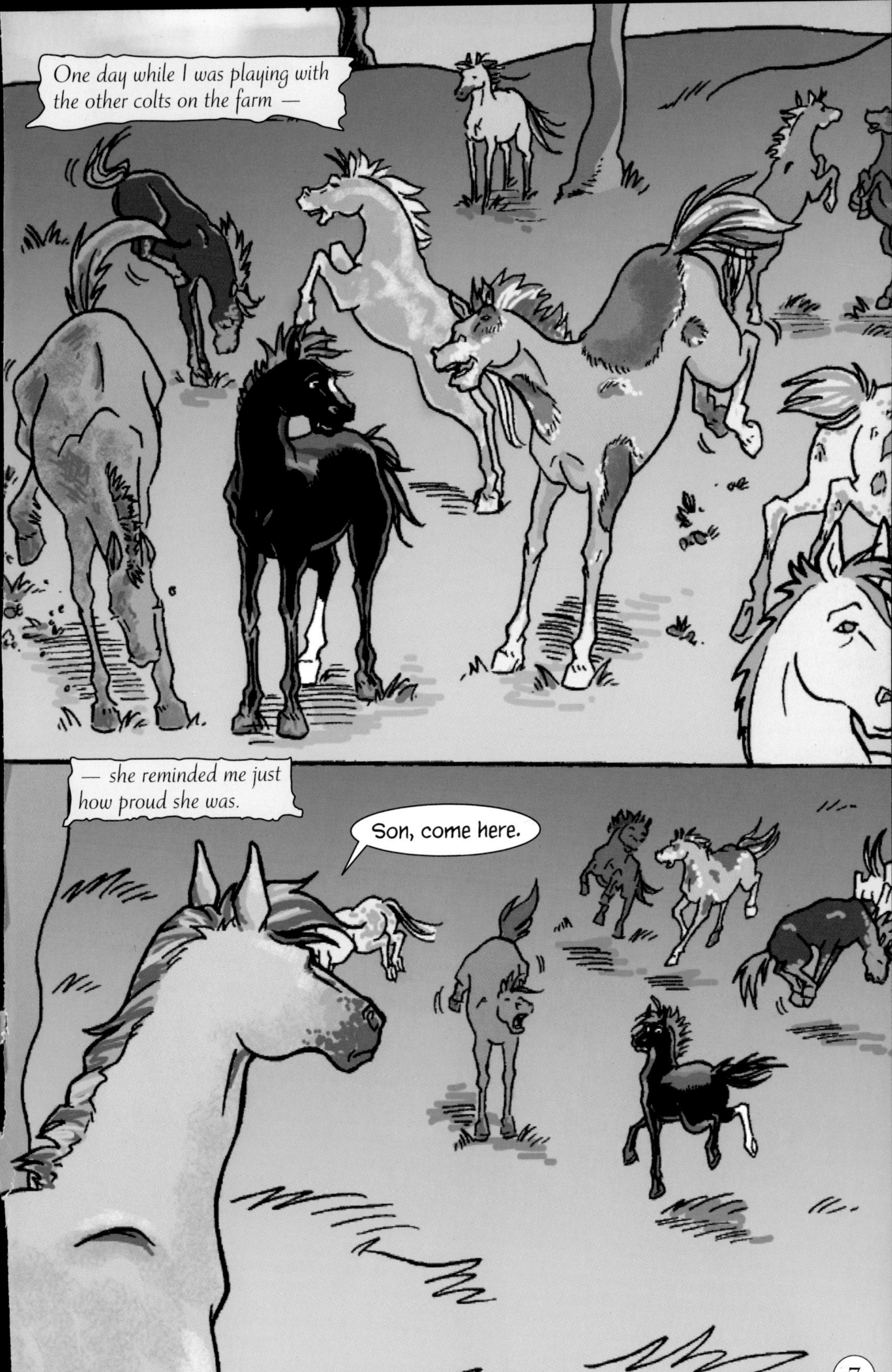
One day while I was playing with the other colts on the farm —
— she reminded me just how proud she was.
Son, come here.

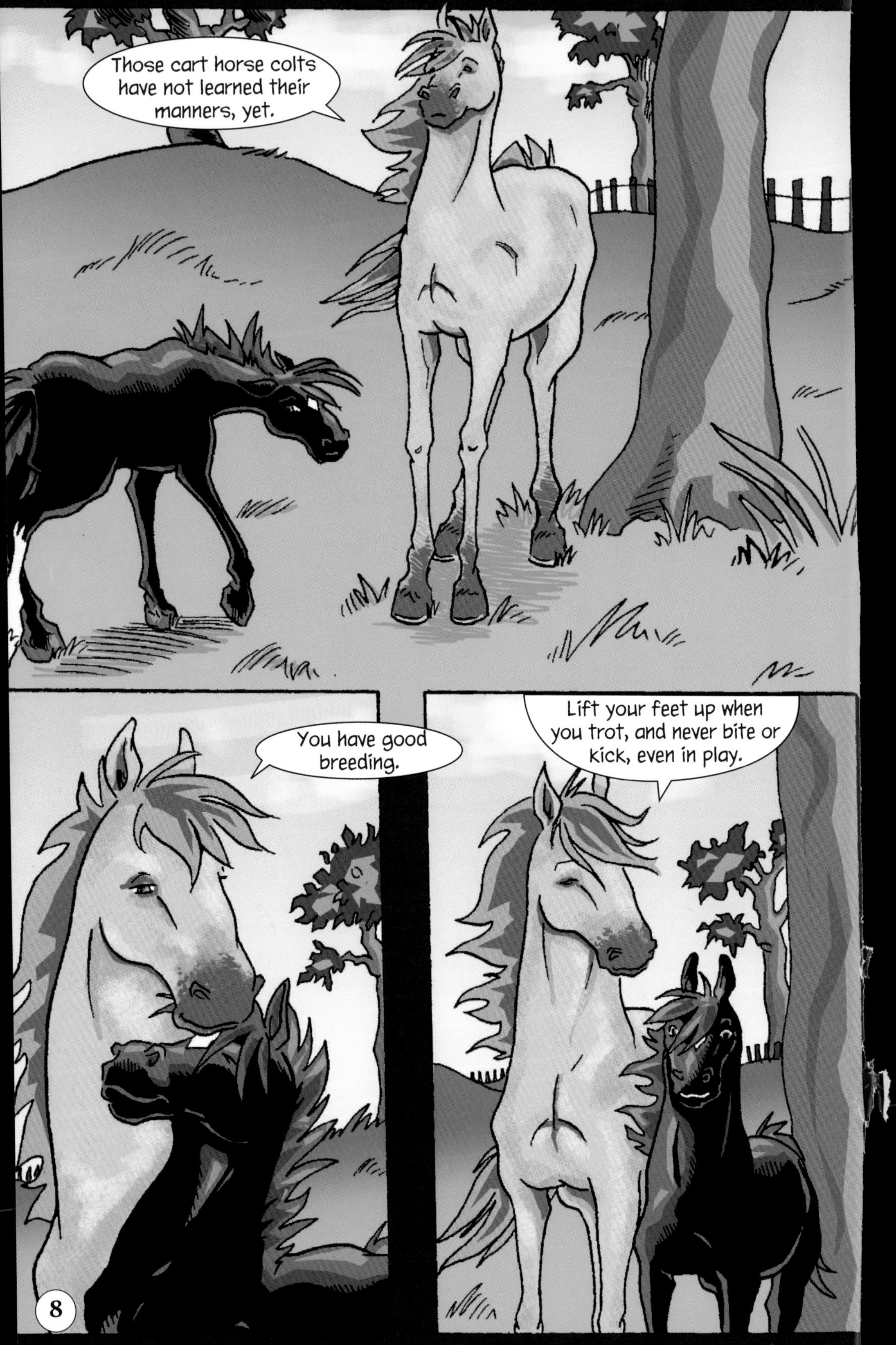
Those cart horse colts have not learned their manners, yet.
You have good breeding.
Lift your feet up when you trot, and never bite or kick, even in play.

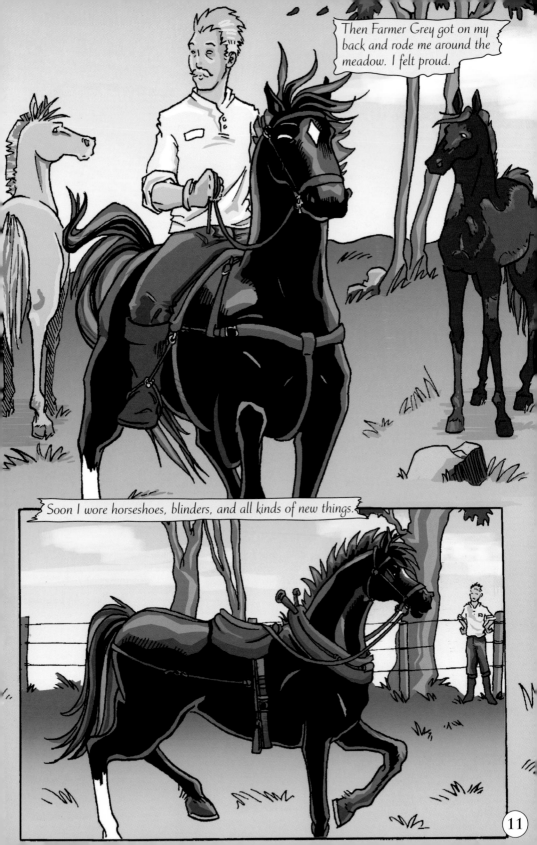

Then Farmer Grey got on my back and rode me around the meadow. I felt proud.

Soon I wore horseshoes, blinders, and all kinds of new things.

11

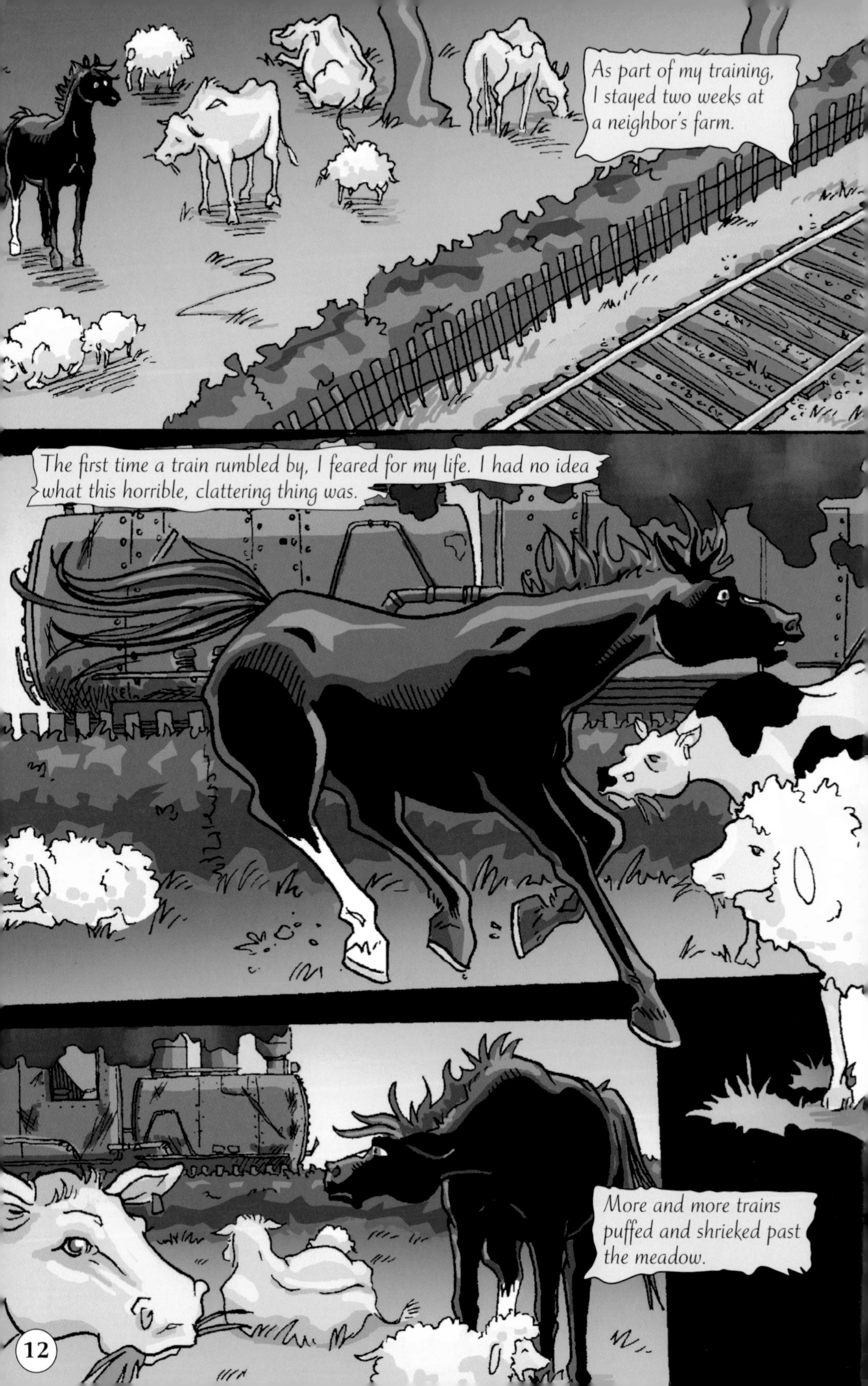
As part of my training, I stayed two weeks at a neighbor's farm.
The first time a train rumbled by, I feared for my life. I had no idea what this horrible, clattering thing was.
More and more trains puffed and shrieked past the meadow.

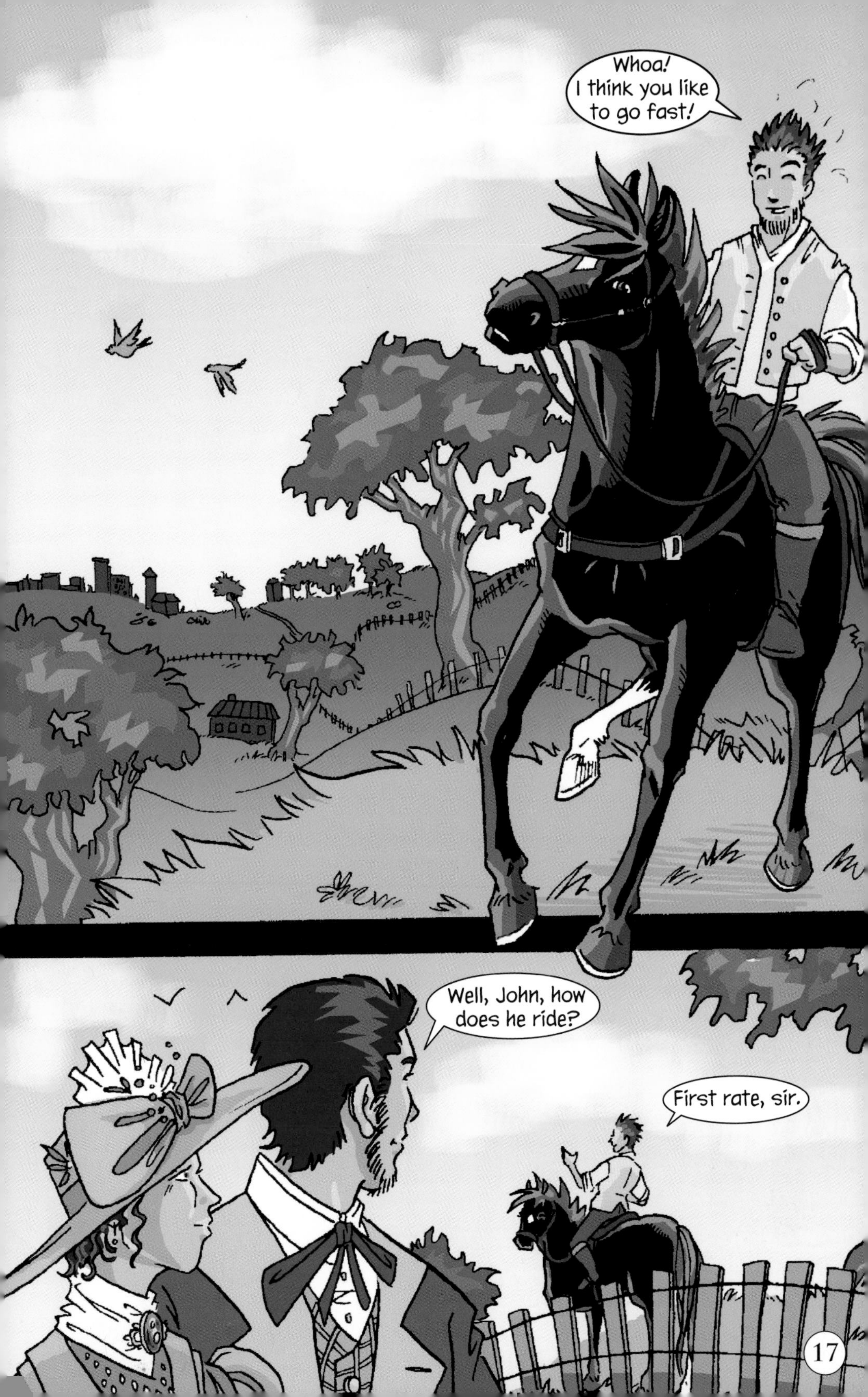
Whoa! I think you like to go fast!
Well, John, how does he ride?
First rate, sir.

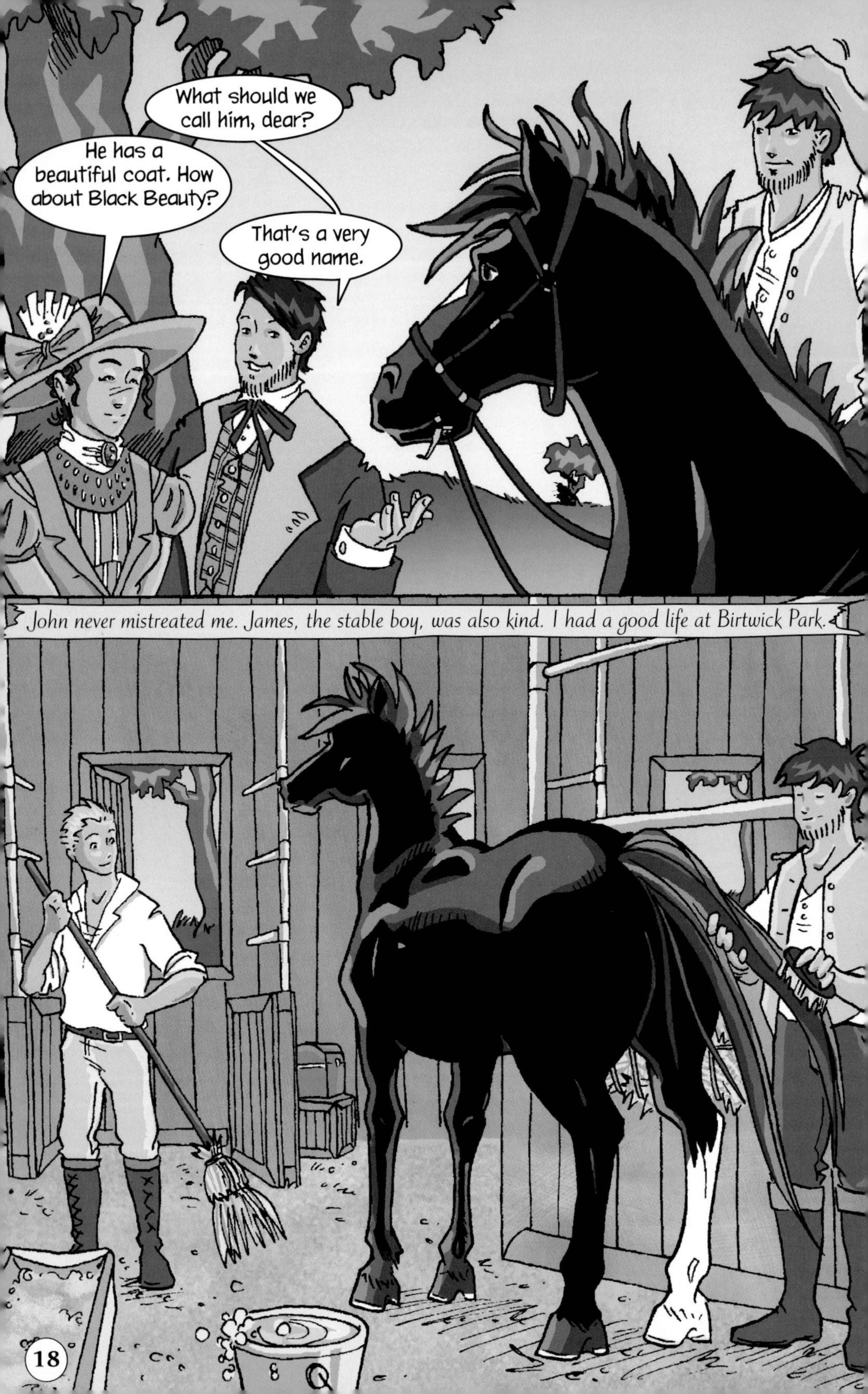
What should we call him, dear?
He has a beautiful coat. How about Black Beauty?
That's a very good name.
John never mistreated me. James, the stable boy, was also kind. I had a good life at Birtwick Park.

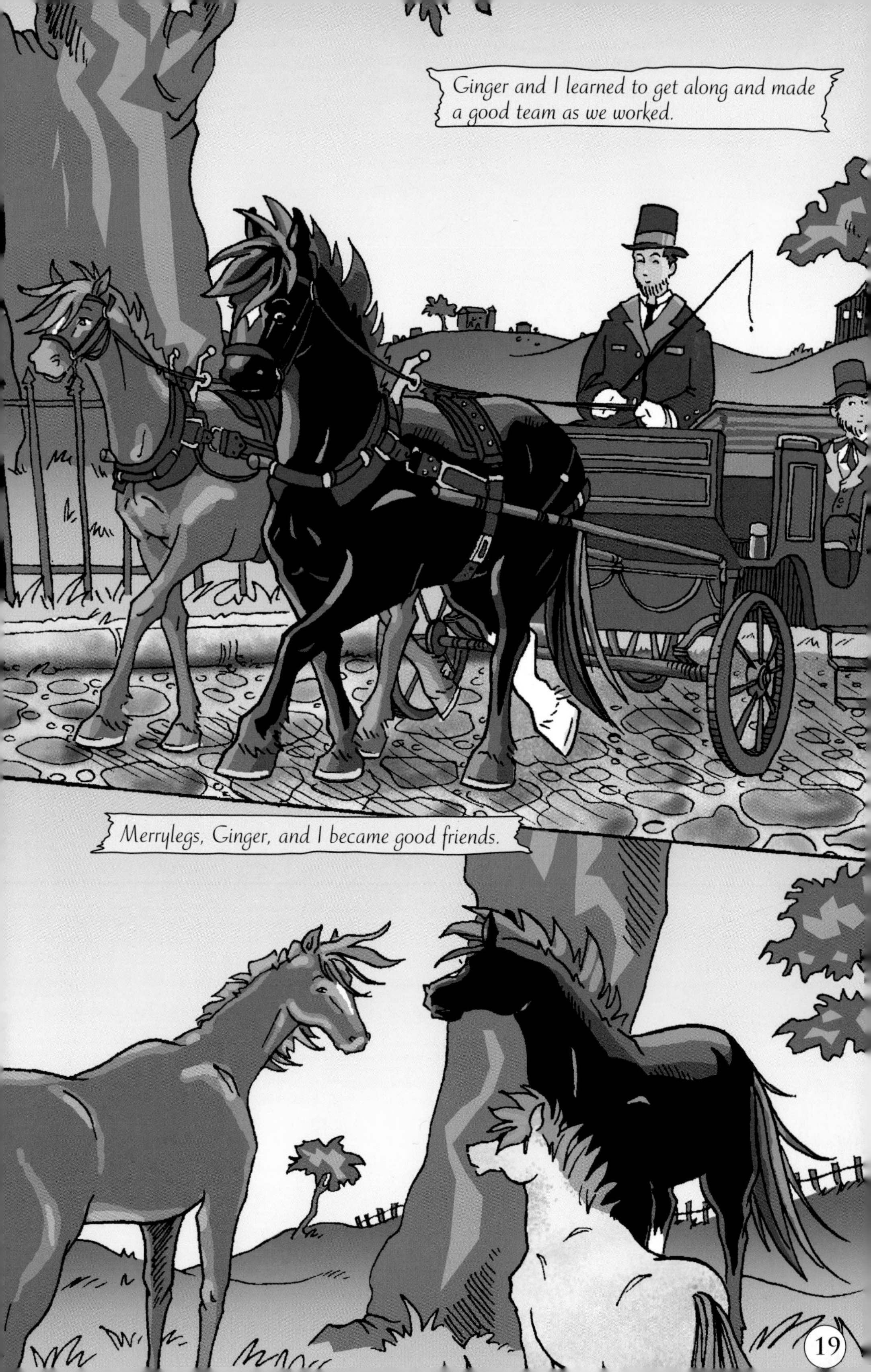
Ginger and I learned to get along and made a good team as we worked.
Merrylegs, Ginger, and I became good friends.

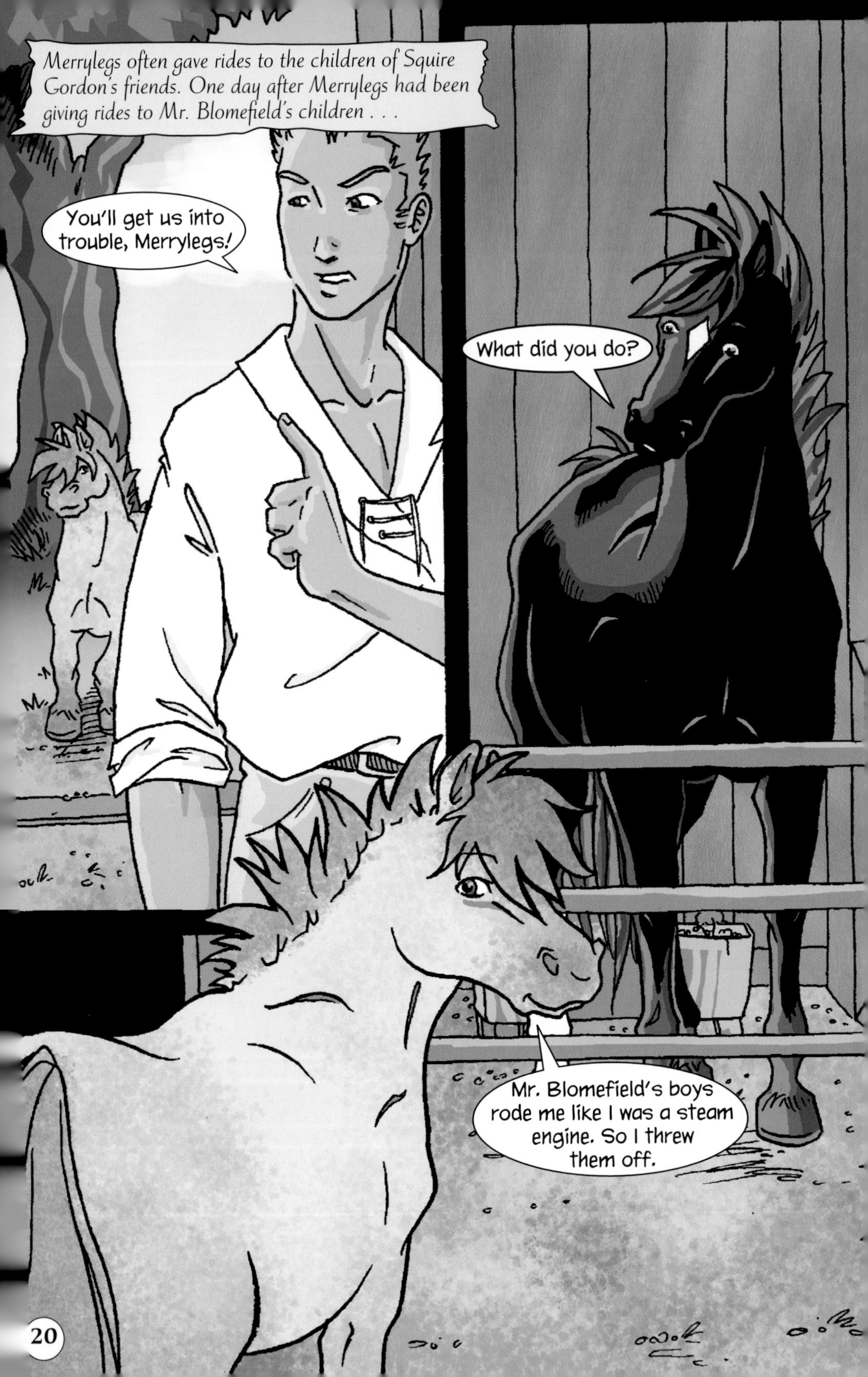
Merrylegs often gave rides to the children of Squire Gordon's friends. One day after Merrylegs had been giving rides to Mr. Blomefield's children . . .
You'll get us into trouble, Merrylegs!
What did you do?
Mr. Blomefield's boys rode me like I was a steam engine. So I threw them off.

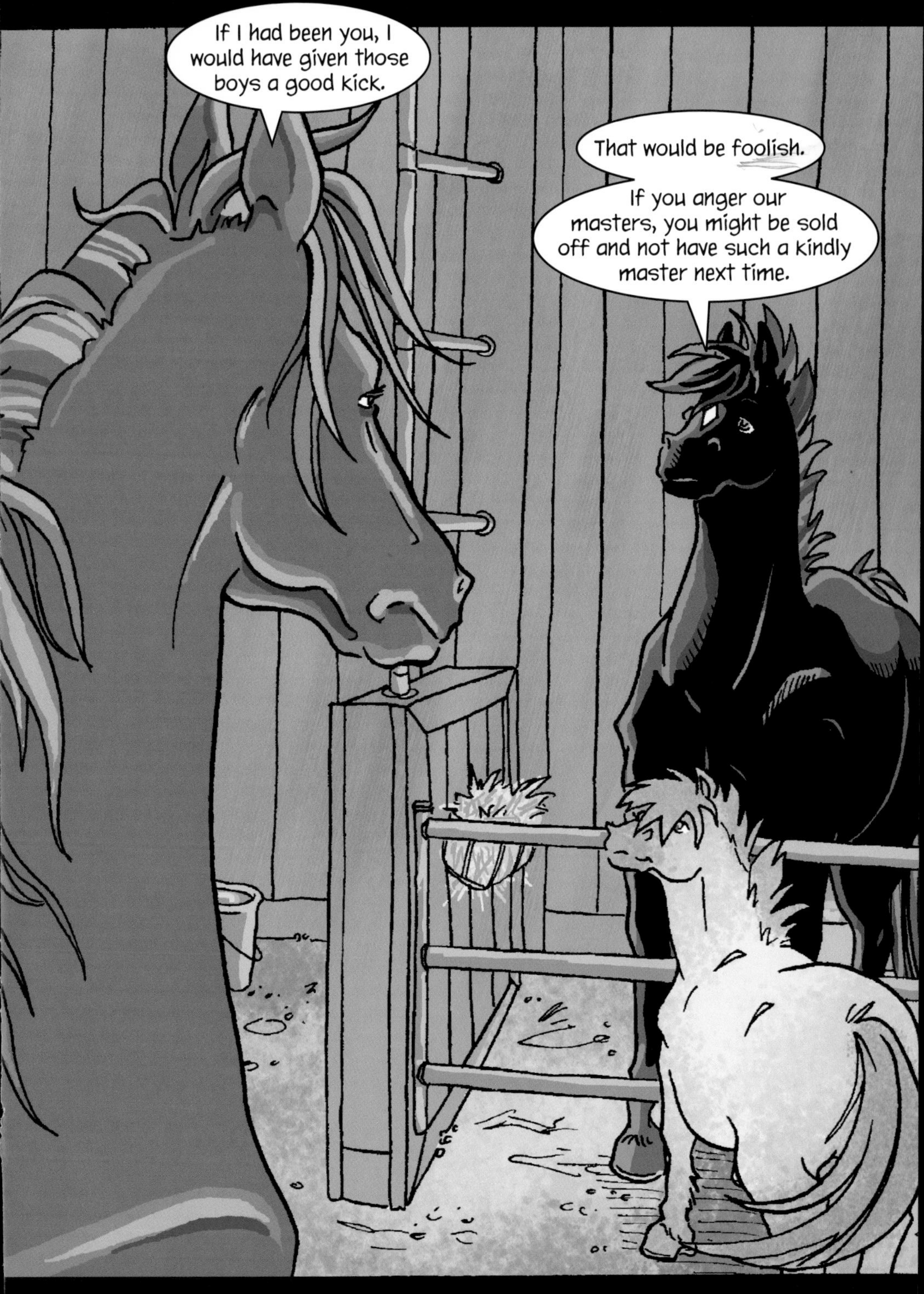
If I had been you, I would have given those boys a good kick.
That would be foolish.
If you anger our masters, you might be sold off and not have such a kindly master next time.

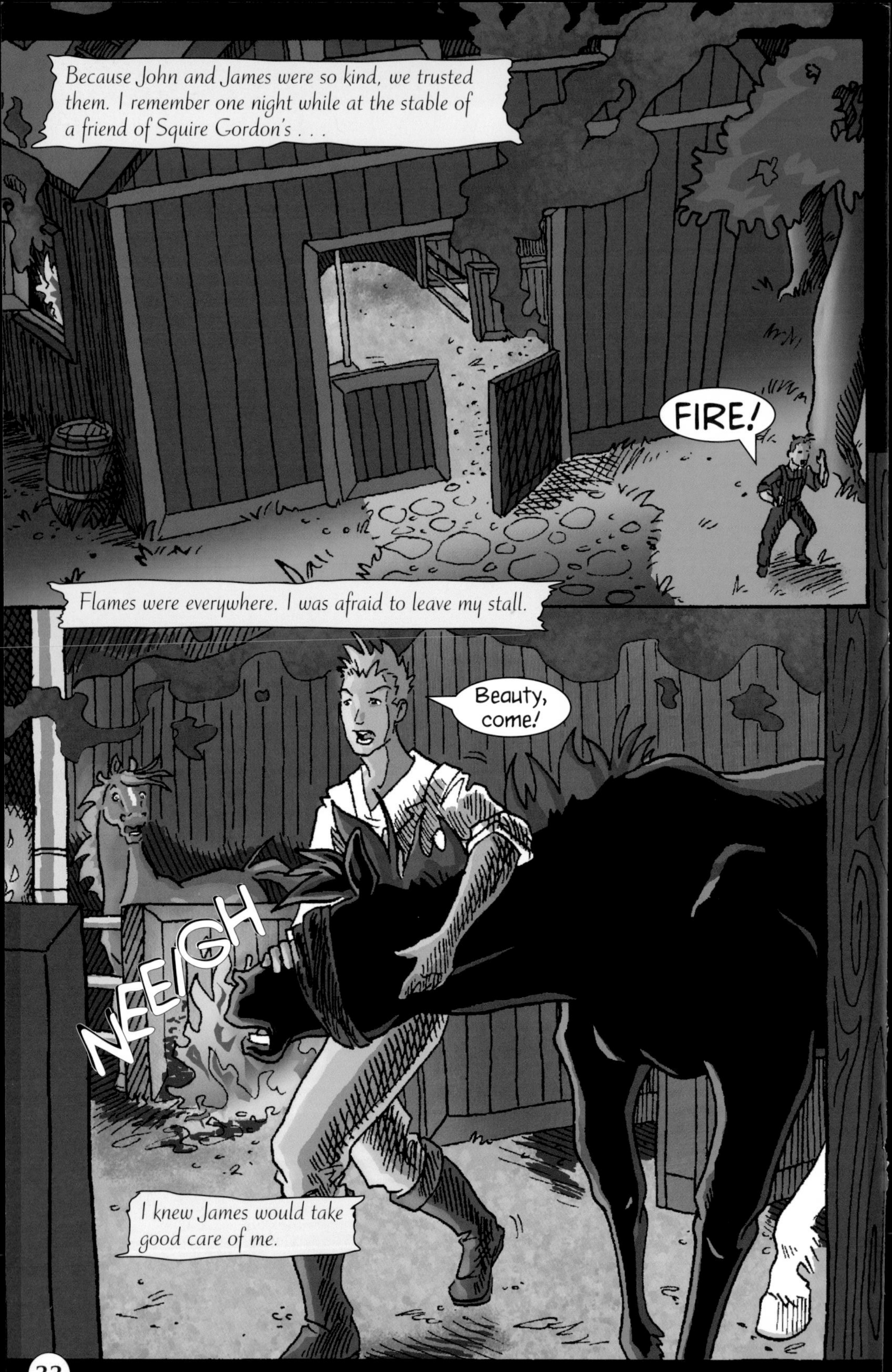

Because John and James were so kind, we trusted them. I remember one night while at the stable of a friend of Squire Gordon's . . .
FIRE!
Flames were everywhere. I was afraid to leave my stall.
Beauty, come!
NEEIGH
I knew James would take good care of me.

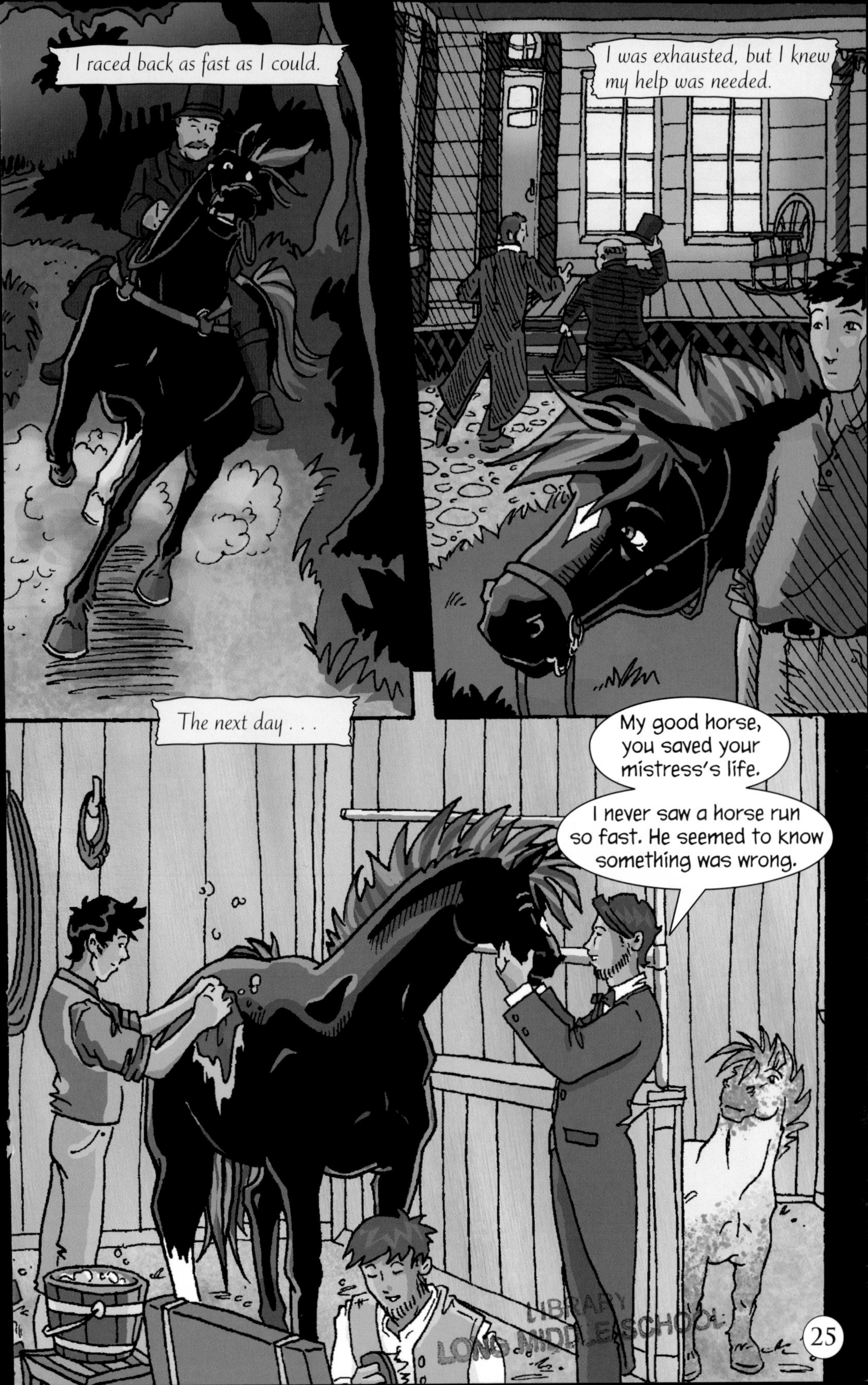
I raced back as fast as I could.
I was exhausted, but I knew my help was needed.
The next day . . .
My good horse, you saved your mistress's life.
I never saw a horse run so fast. He seemed to know something was wrong.

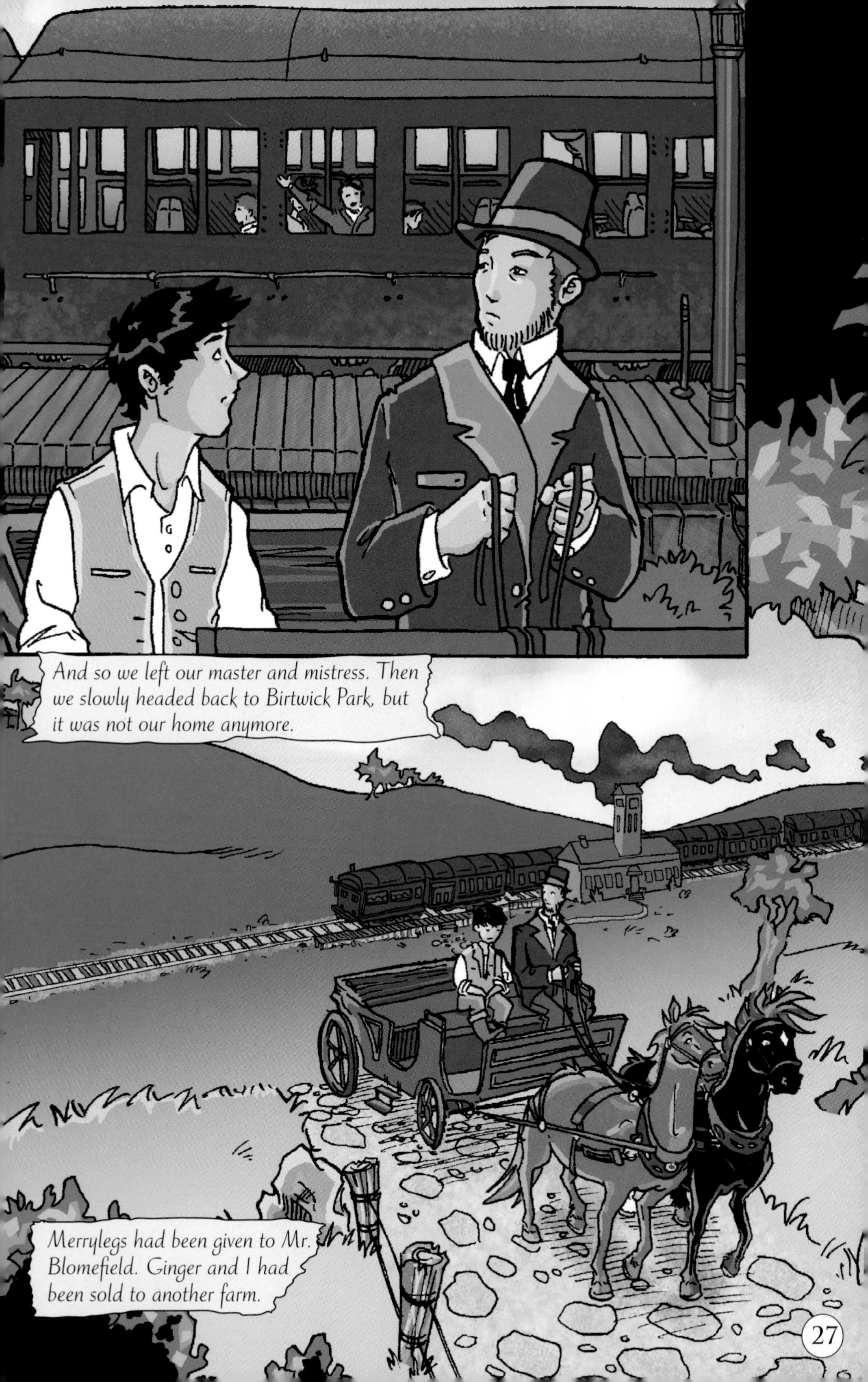
And so we left our master and mistress. Then we slowly headed back to Birtwick Park, but it was not our home anymore.
Merrylegs had been given to Mr. Blomefield. Ginger and I had been sold to another farm.

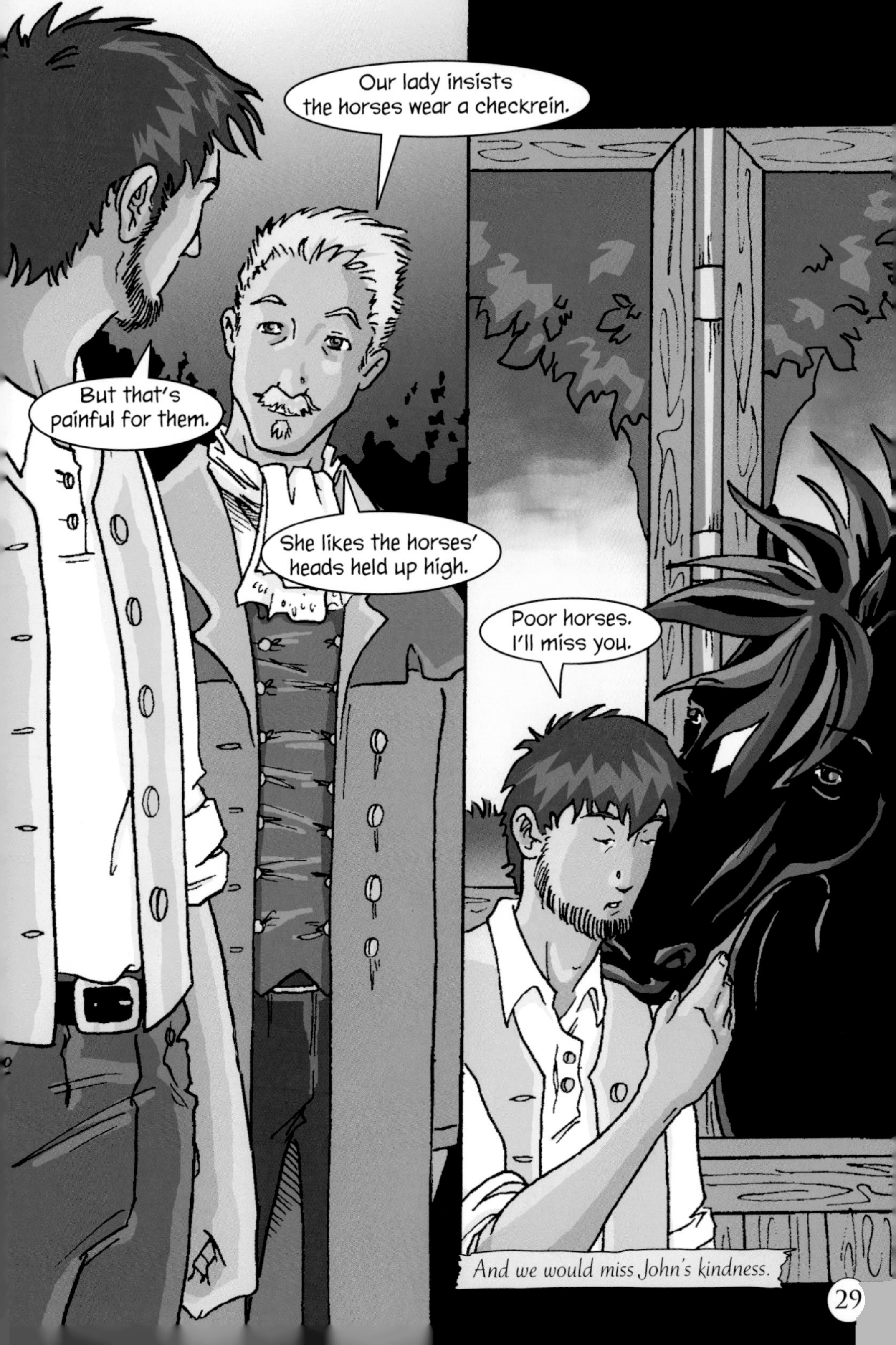
Our lady insists the horses wear a checkrein.
But that's painful for them.
She likes the horses' heads held up high.
Poor horses. I'll miss you.
And we would miss John's kindness.

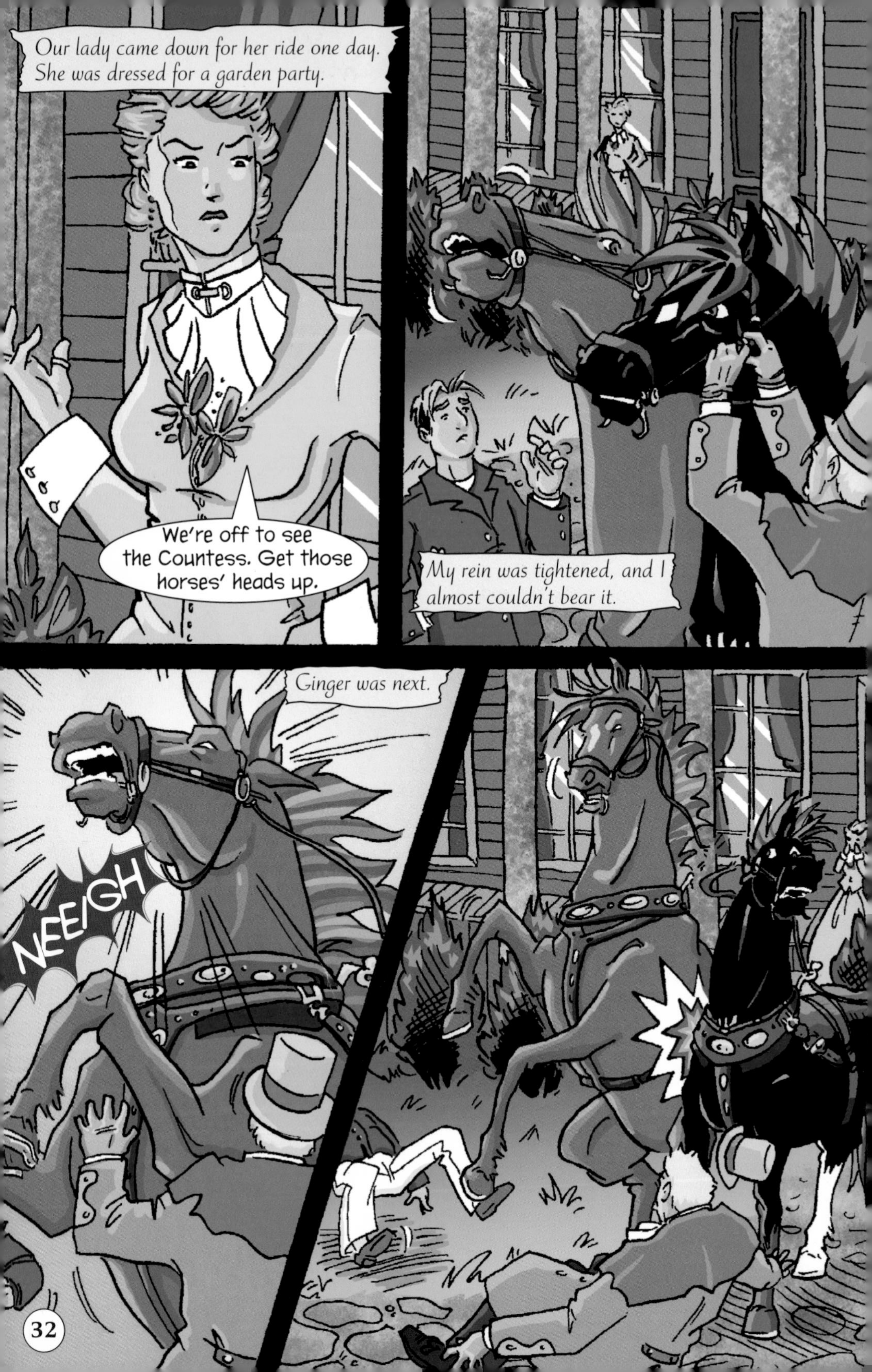
Our lady came down for her ride one day. She was dressed for a garden party.
We're off to see the Countess. Get those horses' heads up.
My rein was tightened, and I almost couldn't bear it.
Ginger was next.
NEEIGH

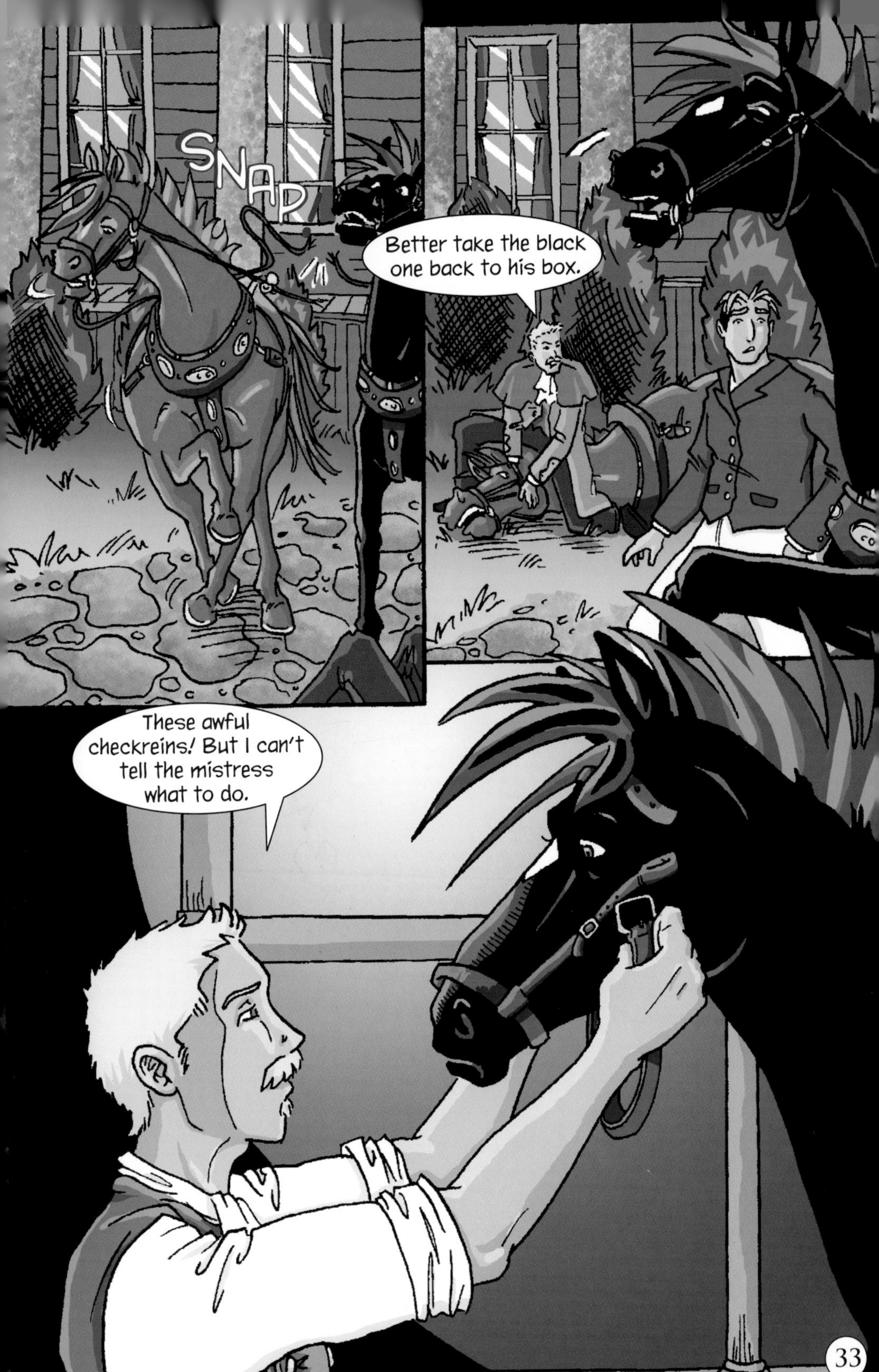
SNAP
Better take the black one back to his box.
These awful checkreins! But I can't tell the mistress what to do.

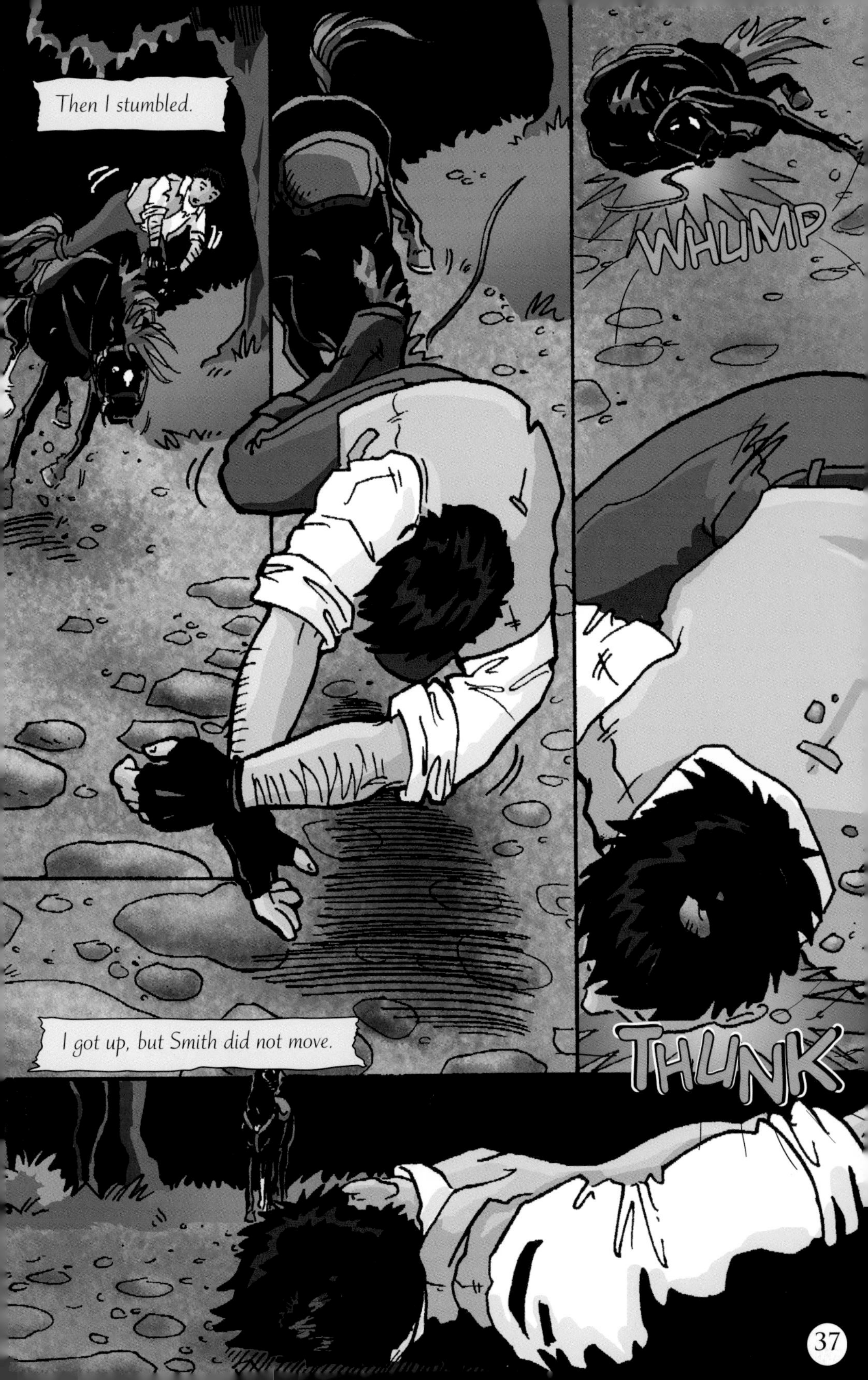
Then I stumbled.
WHUMP
THUNK
I got up, but Smith did not move.

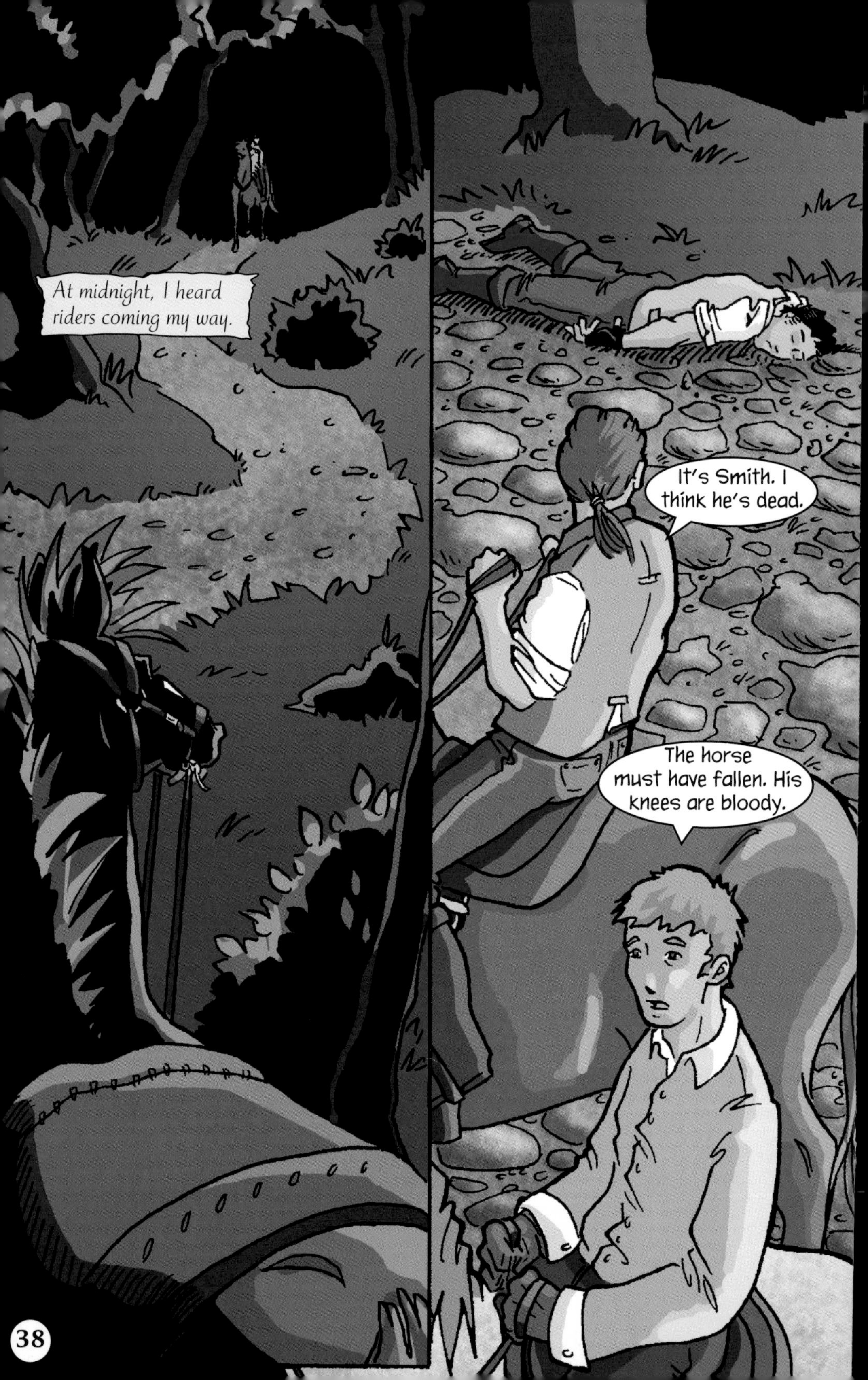
At midnight, I heard riders coming my way.
It's Smith. I think he's dead.
The horse must have fallen. His knees are bloody.

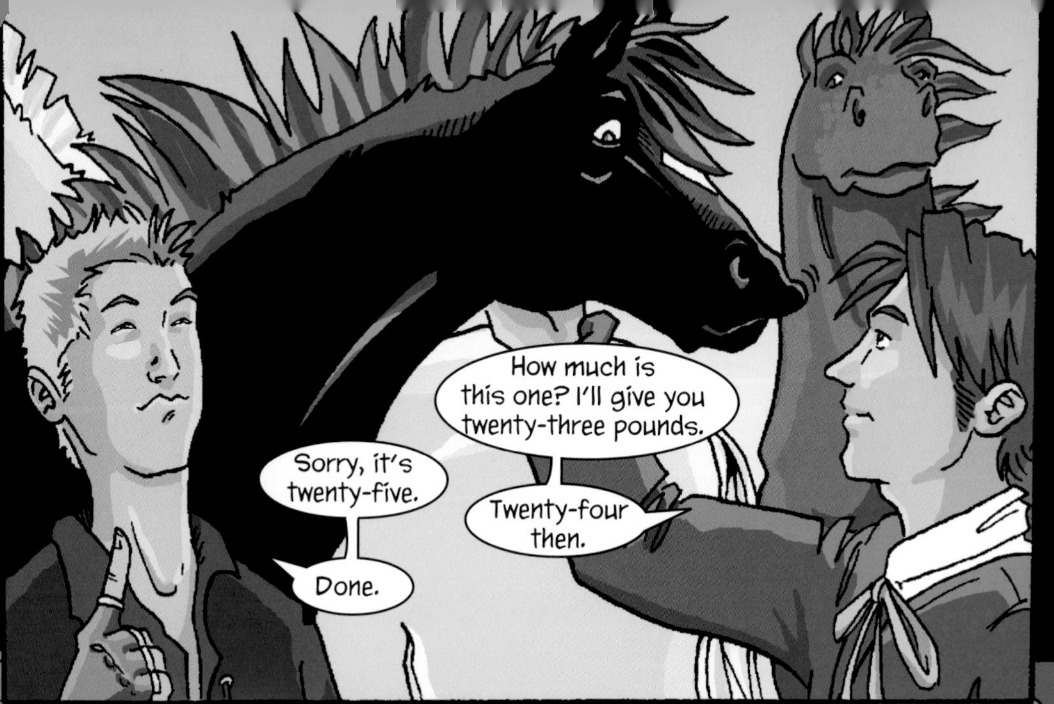
How much is this one? I'll give you twenty-three pounds.
Sorry, it's twenty-five.
Twenty-four then.
Done.

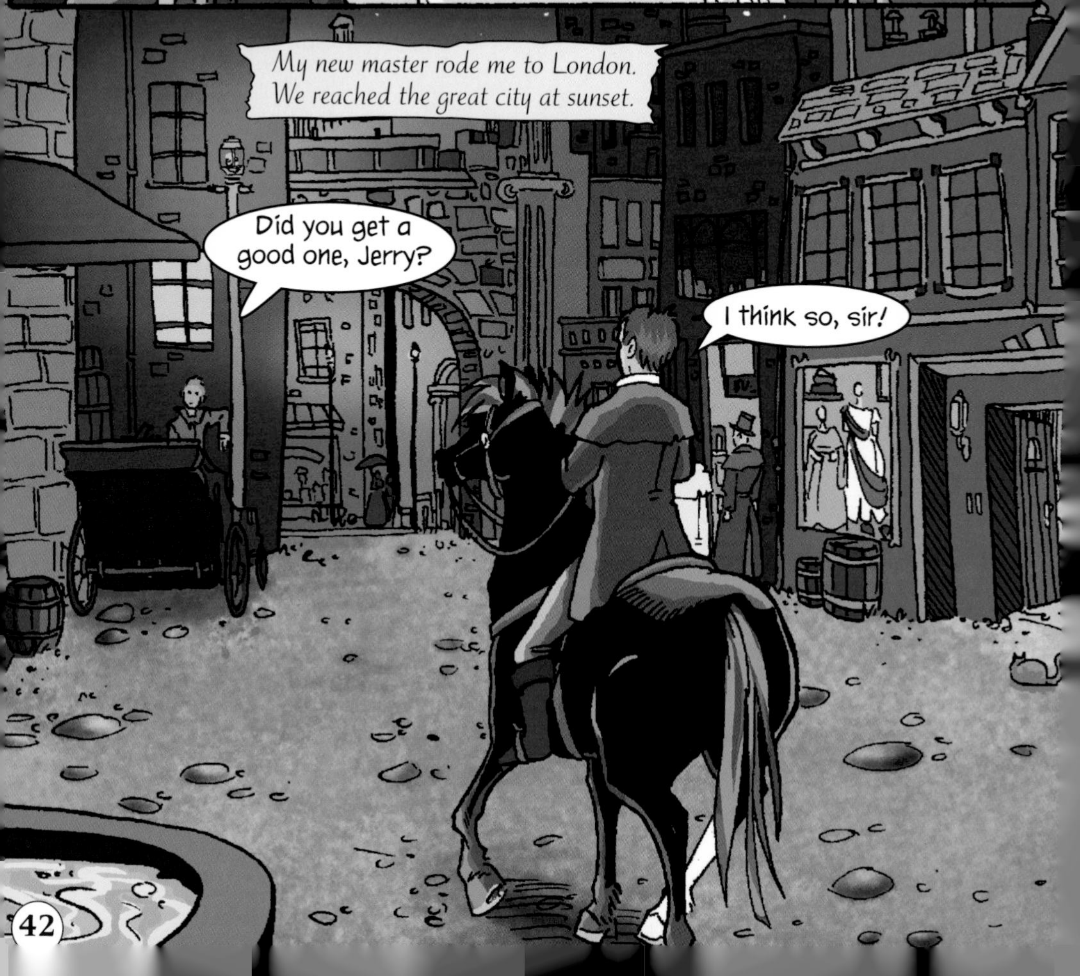
My new master rode me to London. We reached the great city at sunset.
Did you get a good one, Jerry?
I think so, sir!

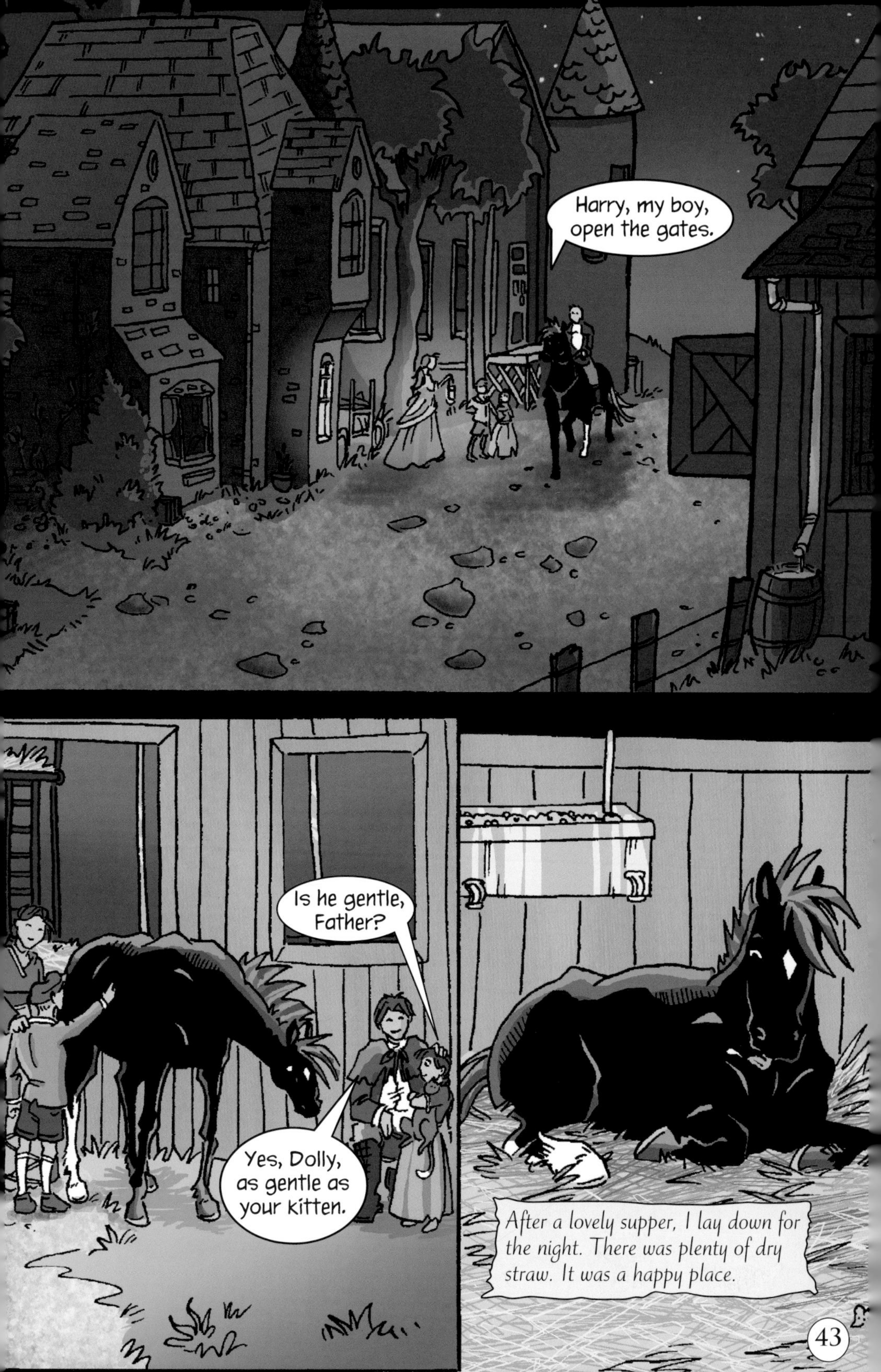
Harry, my boy, open the gates.
Is he gentle, Father?
Yes, Dolly, as gentle as your kitten.
After a lovely supper, I lay down for the night. There was plenty of dry straw. It was a happy place.

Chapter 4 ★ A LONDON CAB HORSE

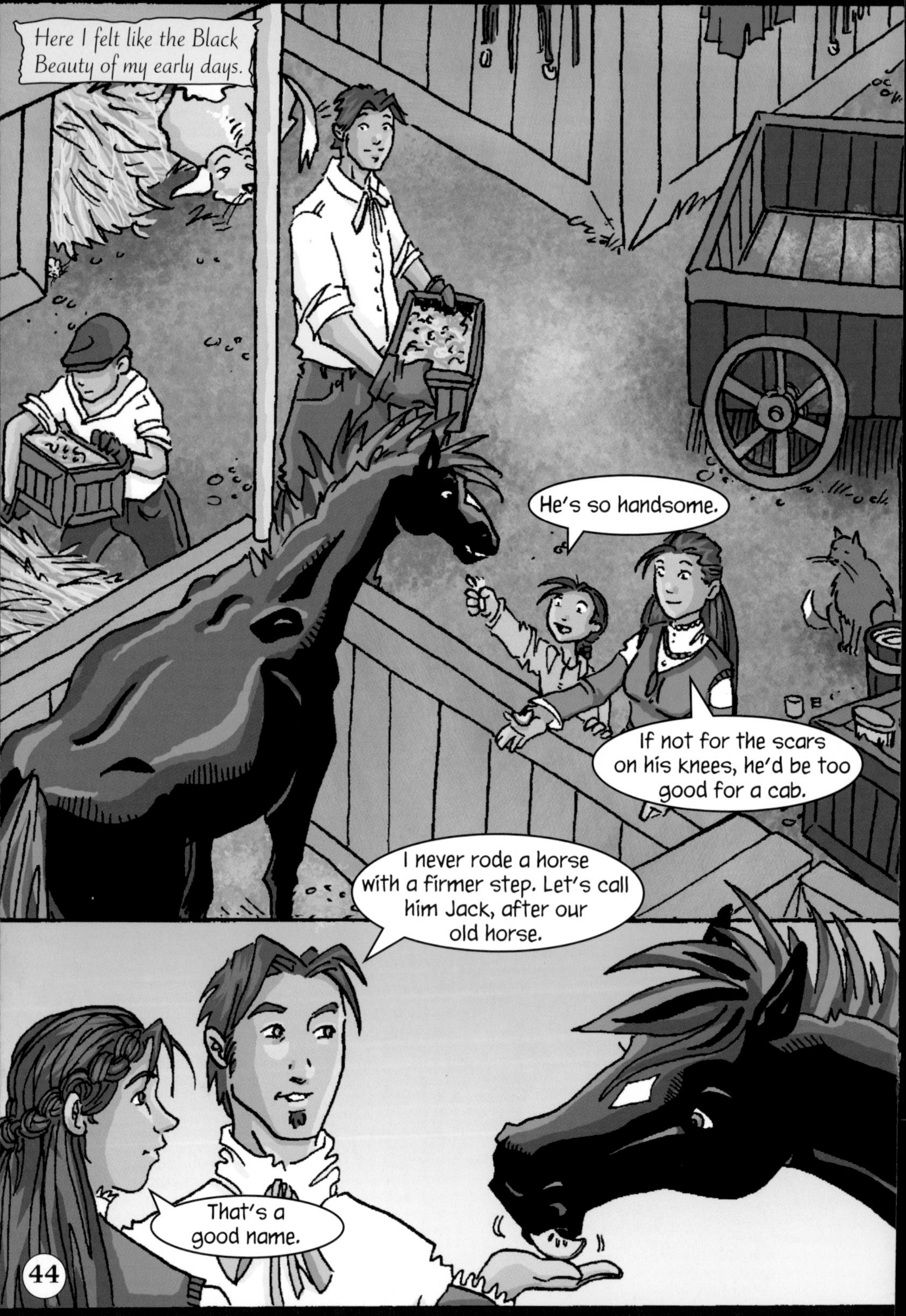
Here I felt like the Black Beauty of my early days.
He's so handsome.
If not for the scars on his knees, he'd be too good for a cab.
I never rode a horse with a firmer step. Let's call him Jack, after our old horse.
That's a good name.

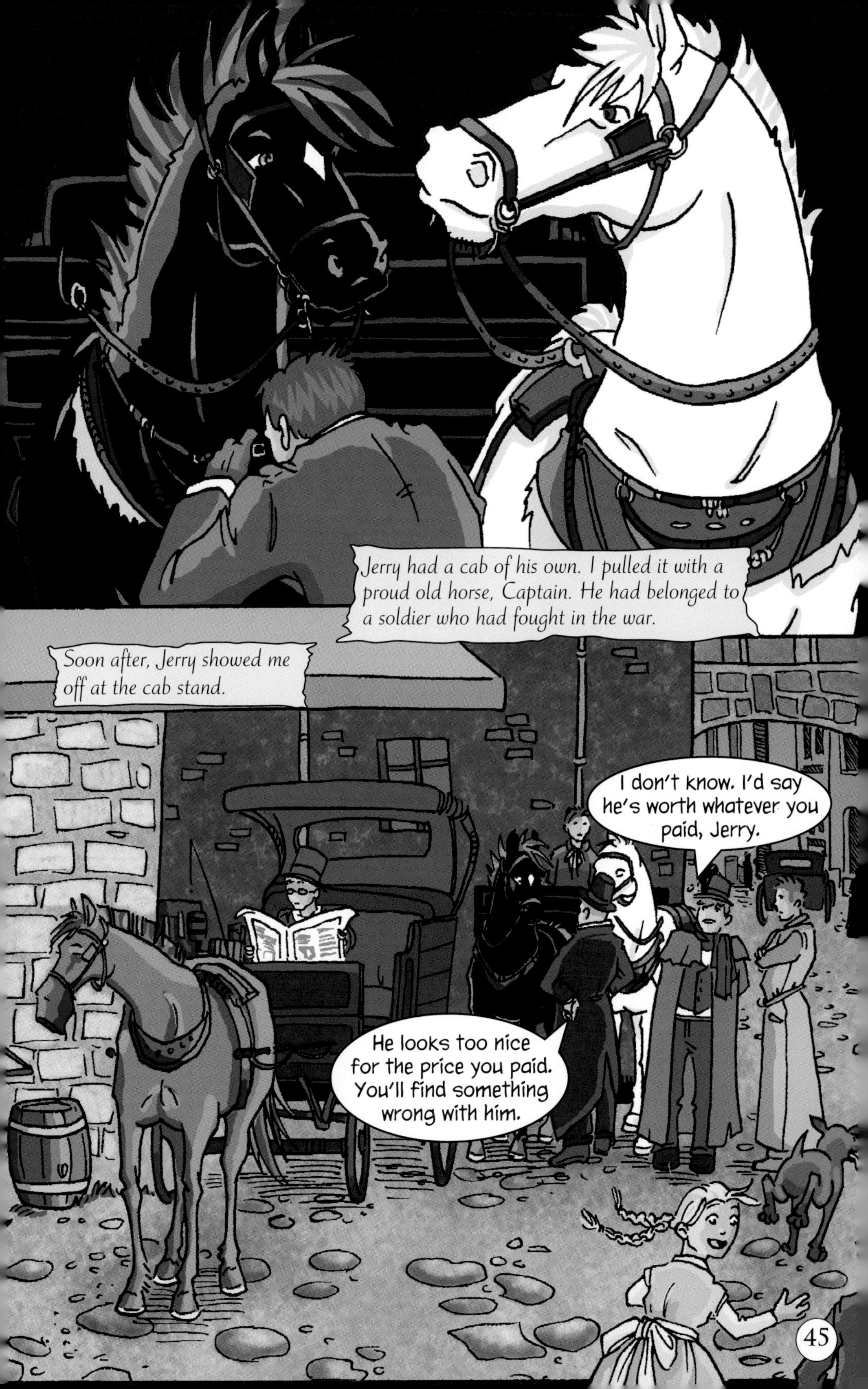
Jerry had a cab of his own. I pulled it with a proud old horse, Captain. He had belonged to a soldier who had fought in the war.
Soon after, Jerry showed me off at the cab stand.
I don't know. I'd say he's worth whatever you paid, Jerry.
He looks too nice for the price you paid. You'll find something wrong with him.

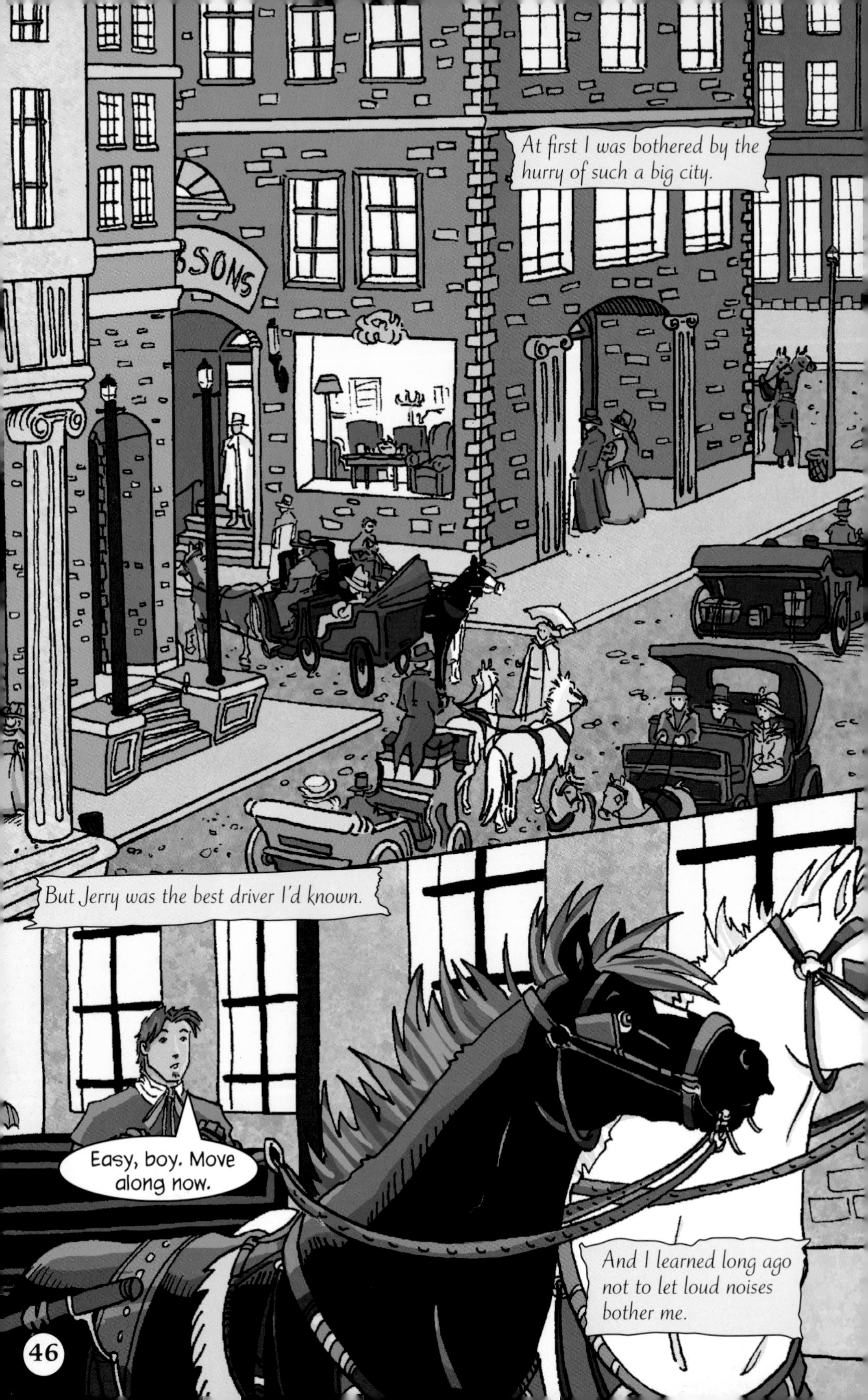
At first I was bothered by the hurry of such a big city.
But Jerry was the best driver I'd known.
Easy, boy. Move along now.
And I learned long ago not to let loud noises bother me.

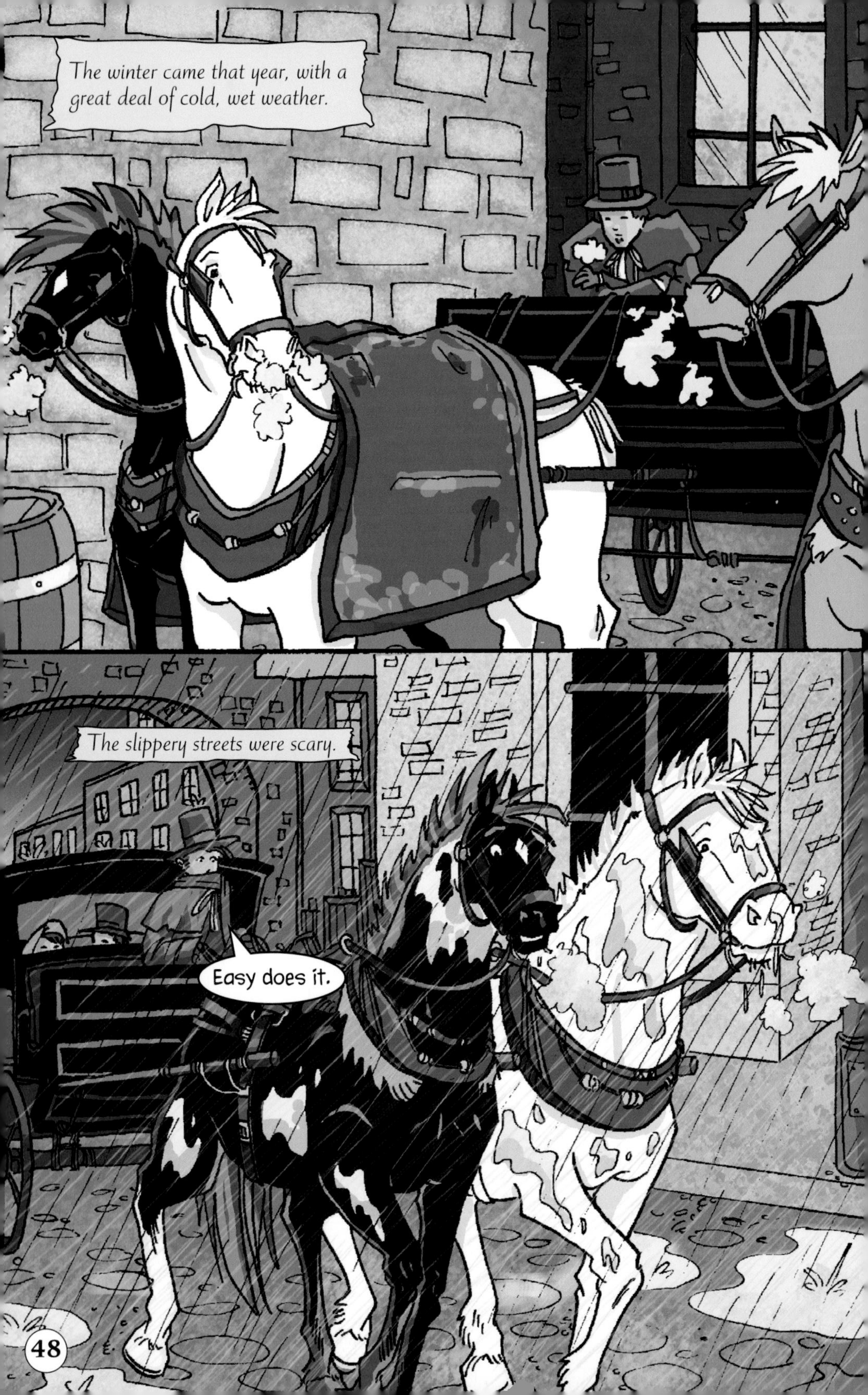
The winter came that year, with a great deal of cold, wet weather.
The slippery streets were scary.
Easy does it.

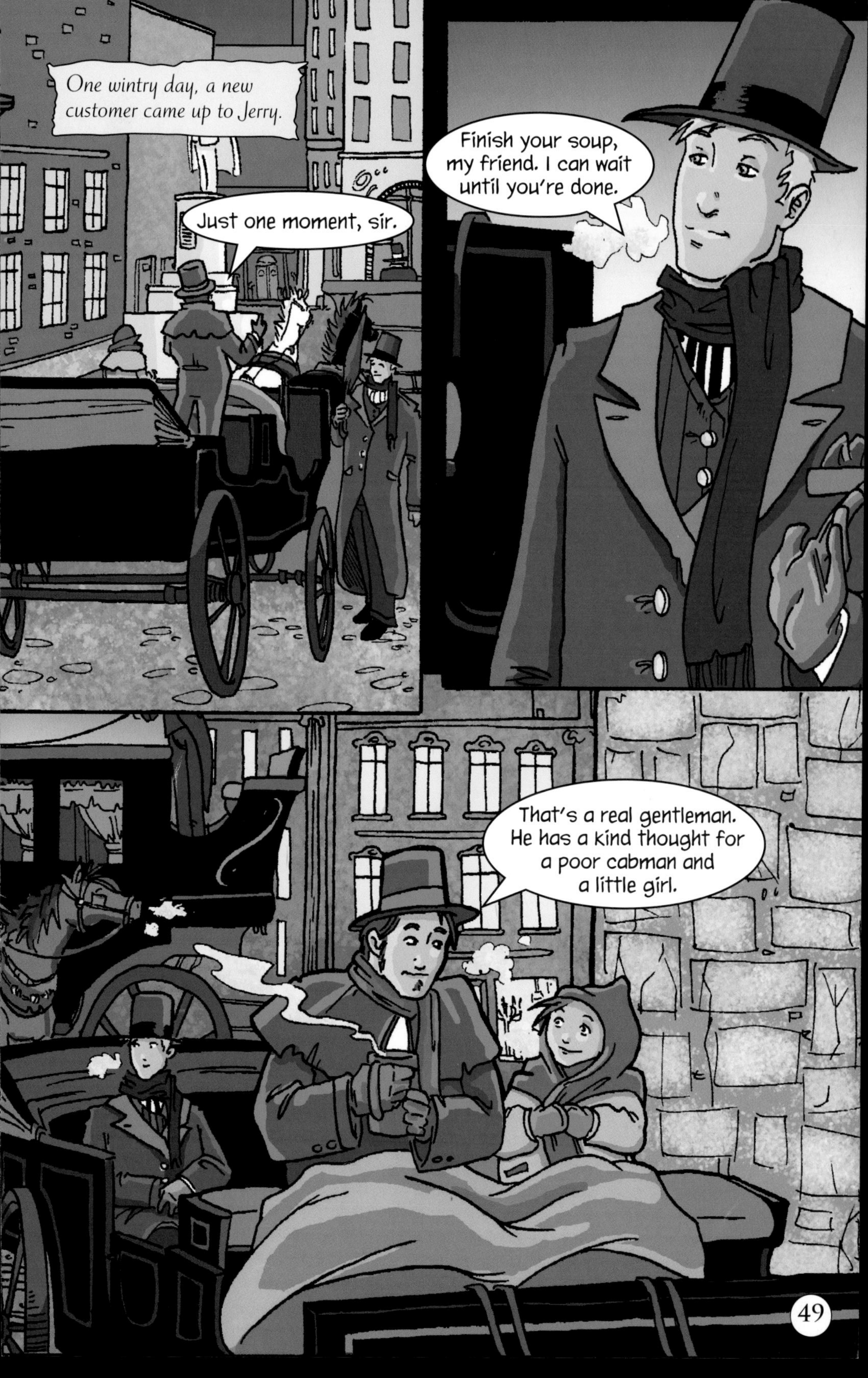
One wintry day, a new customer came up to Jerry.
Just one moment, sir.
Finish your soup, my friend. I can wait until you're done.
That's a real gentleman. He has a kind thought for a poor cabman and a little girl.

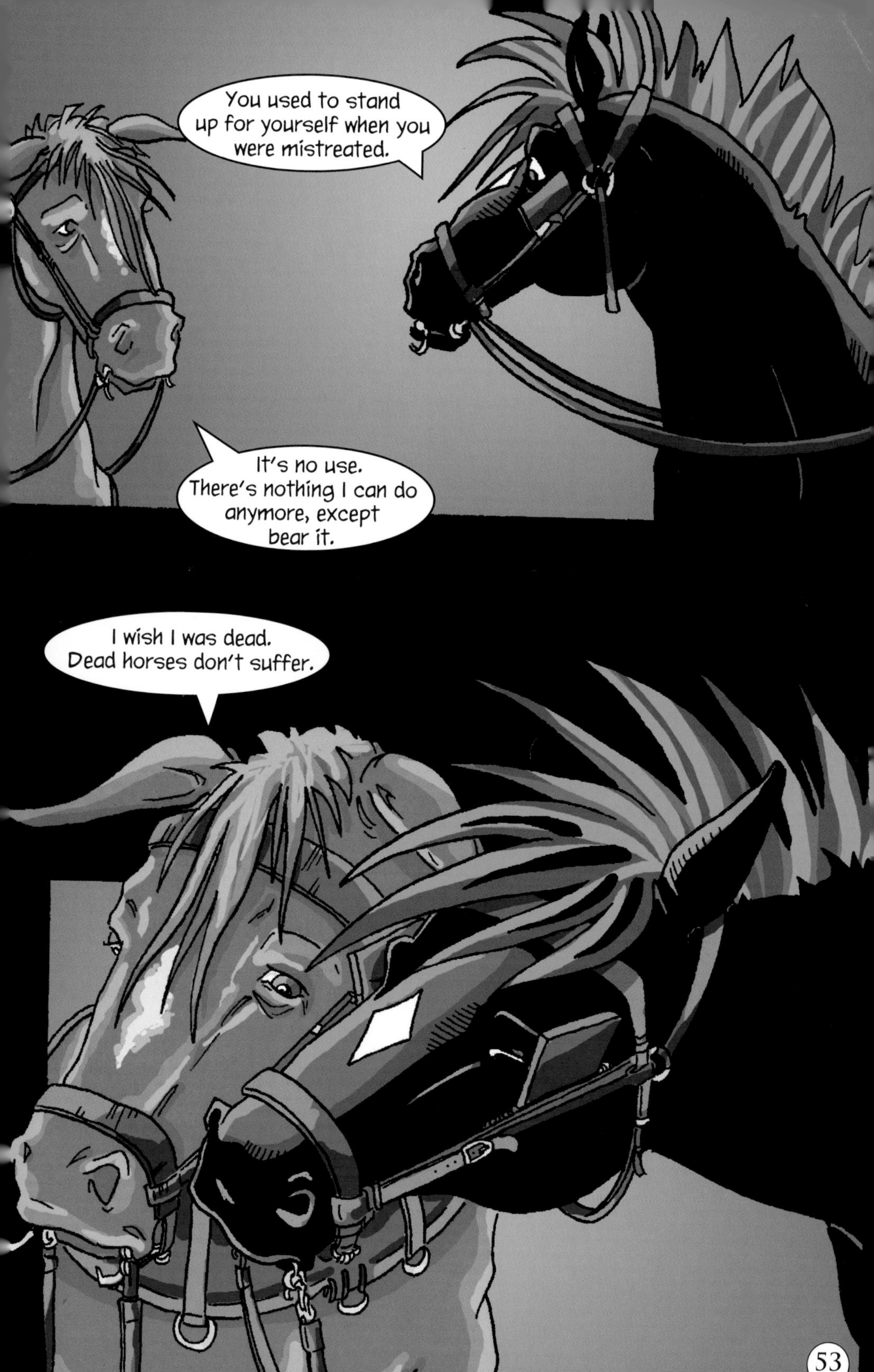
You used to stand up for yourself when you were mistreated.
It's no use. There's nothing I can do anymore, except bear it.
I wish I was dead. Dead horses don't suffer.

With a tug from her driver, Ginger drove off.
Farewell, Black Beauty.

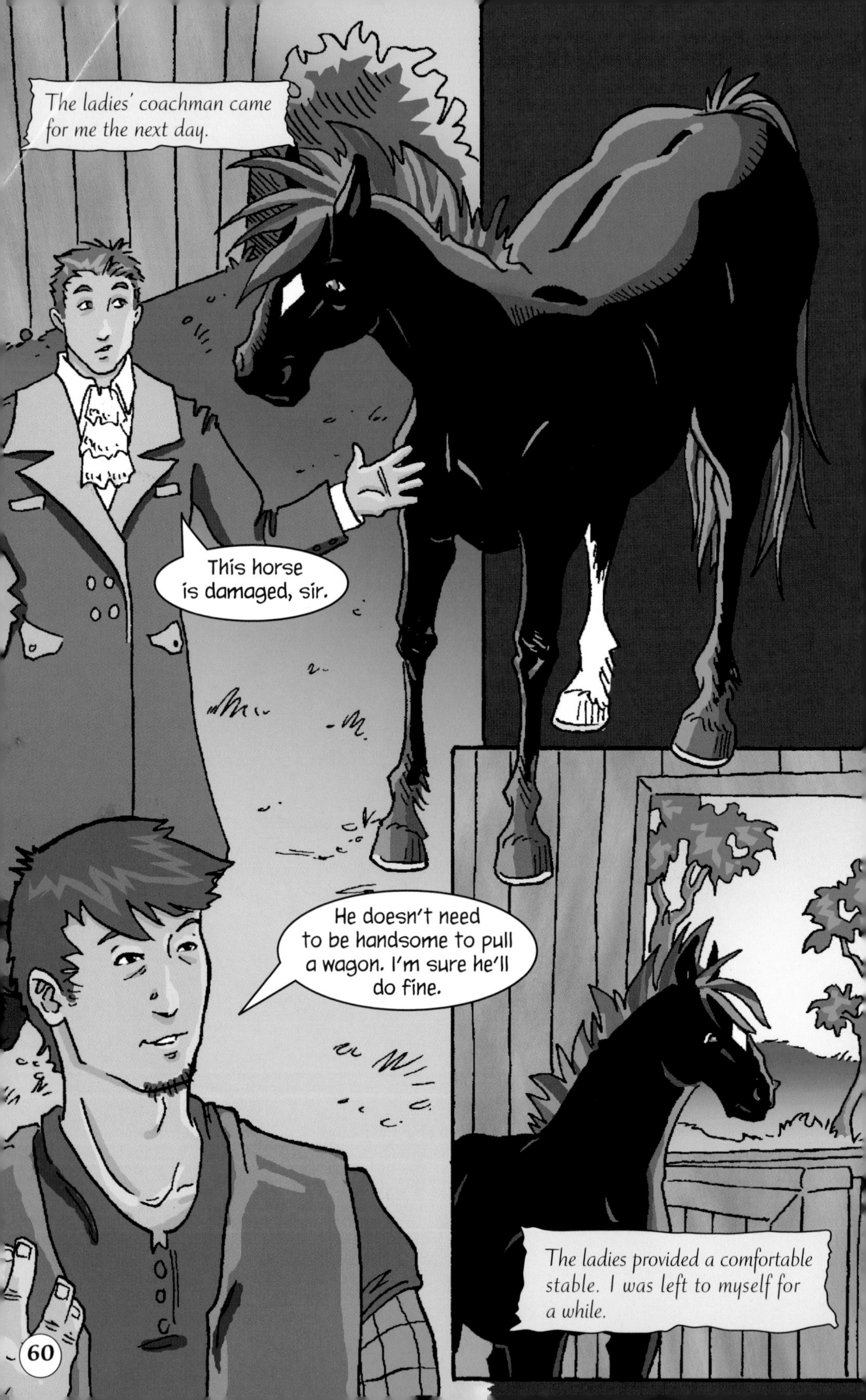
The ladies' coachman came for me the next day.
This horse is damaged, sir.
He doesn't need to be handsome to pull a wagon. I'm sure he'll do fine.
The ladies provided a comfortable stable. I was left to myself for a while.

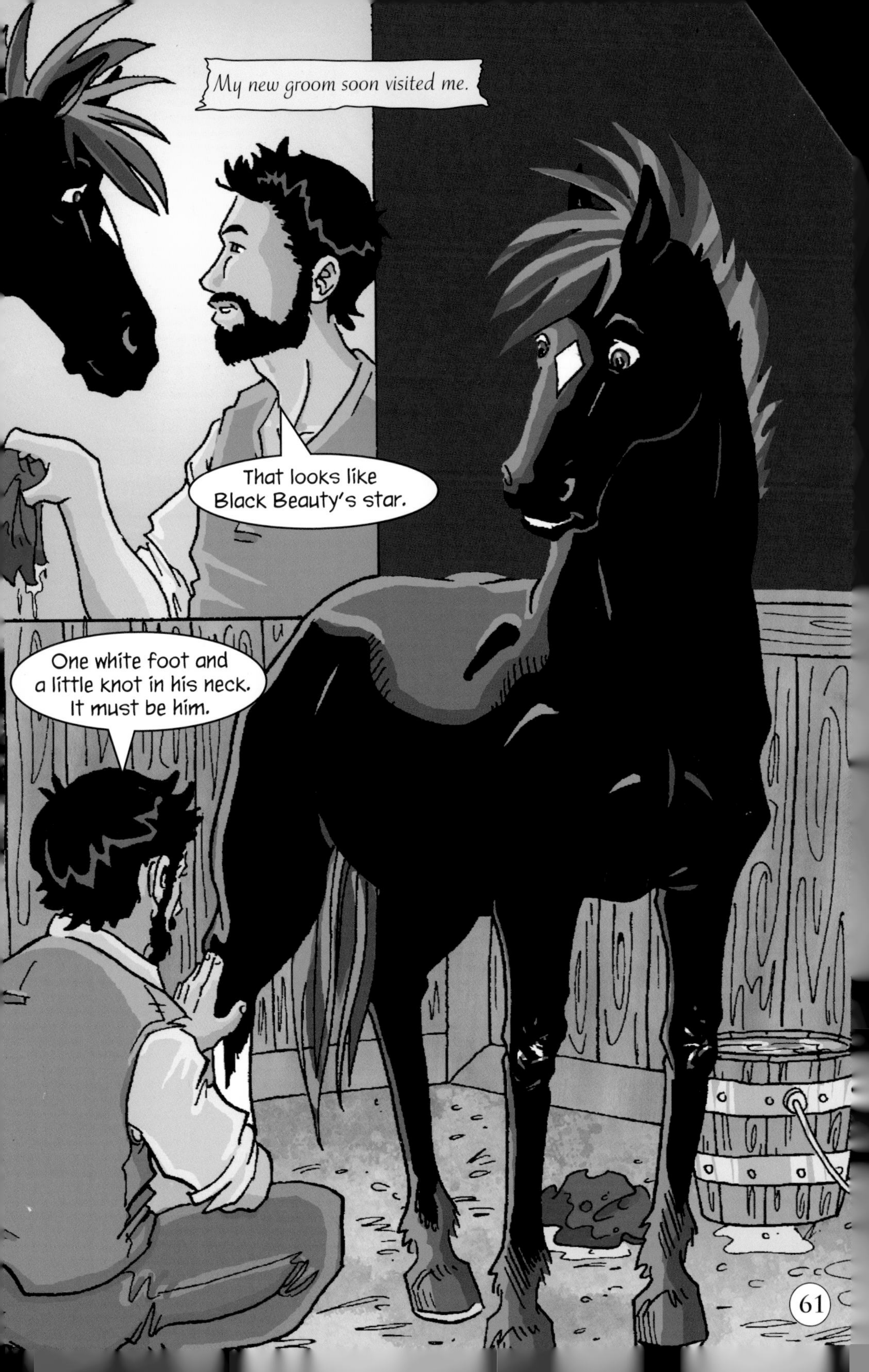
My new groom soon visited me.
That looks like Black Beauty's star.
One white foot and a little knot in his neck. It must be him.

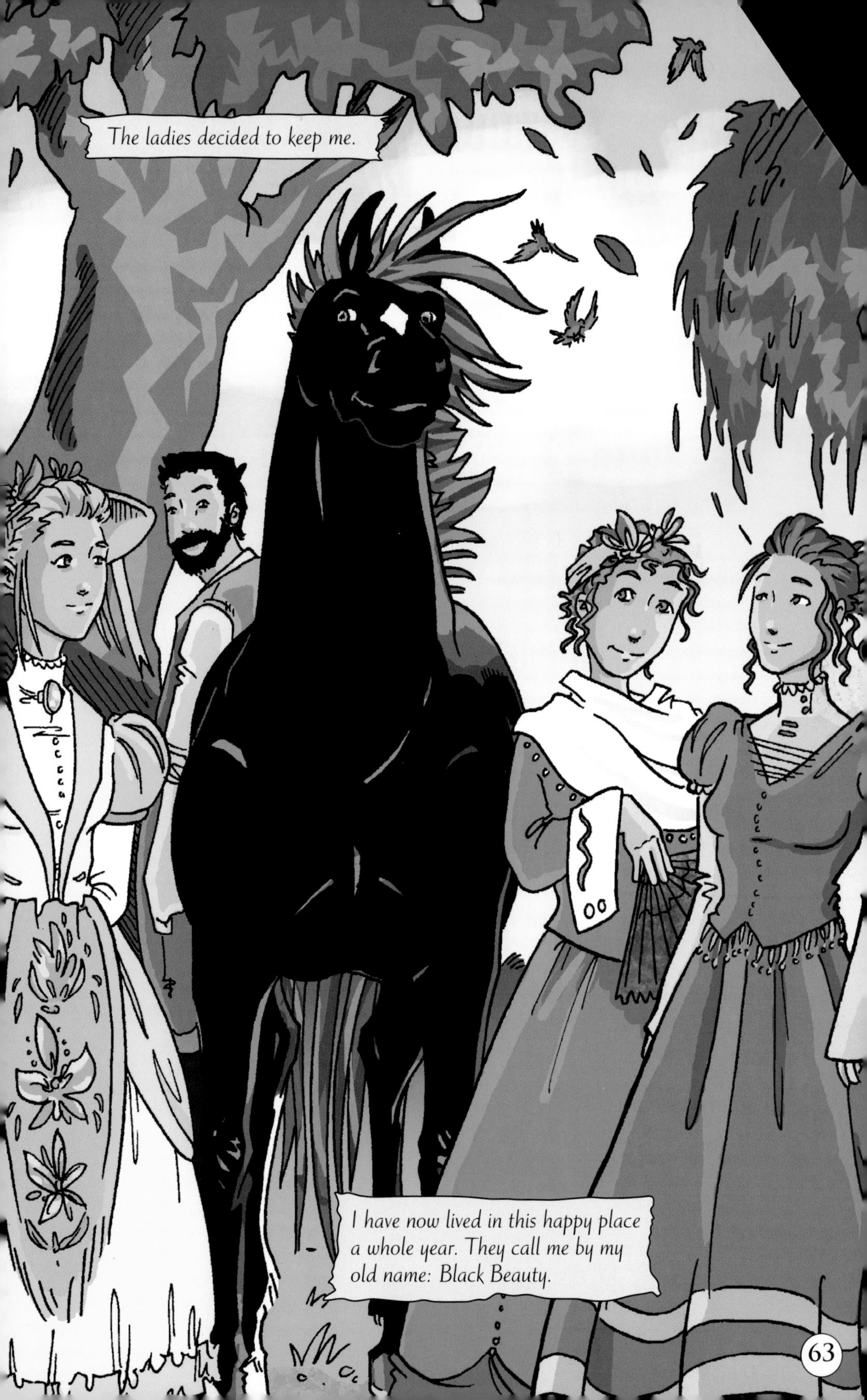
The ladies decided to keep me.
I have now lived in this happy place a whole year. They call me by my old name: Black Beauty.

About Anna Sewell

Anna Sewell was born in 1820 in England. Around the age of 14, Sewell fell and injured her ankles. They didn't heal properly. From then on, she had trouble walking and relied on horses to take her where she needed to go. She loved horses and was grateful for them. Sewell was shocked to see how cruelly some people treated her favorite animal.

In 1871, Sewell was told she had only a short time to live. She decided to write a book that would show the kind and loving nature of horses. That book, the only one she ever wrote, was *Black Beauty*. It has been considered a classic since it was published in 1877.

About the Author

L. L. Owens was born in Iowa and now lives in Seattle, Washington, with her husband. She has written more than 45 books, and she enjoys visiting classrooms to talk about her writing. She likes listening to music, cooking, and exploring the Pacific Northwest.

About the Illustrator

When she was younger, Jennifer Tanner loved to draw humorous comics about dogs who went on spectacular adventures through time and space, meeting alien creatures along the way. Today she spends her time illustrating many comic book stories.

GLOSSARY

colts (KOLTS) — young male horses

damaged (DAM-ijd) — broken or unable to heal

Duchess (DUTCH-iss) — the name of Black Beauty's mother, who was named for a duchess, the wife of a duke

filly (FILL-ee) — a young female horse

ignore (igg-NOR) — to not notice something or pretend that something didn't happen

lord (LORD) — a person who had a royal birth or had power over others

pounds (POUNDZ) — units of money used in England

scolded (SKOLD-id) — told someone that they did something wrong, often in a mean way

squire (SKWIRE) — a country gentleman

stall (STAWL) — a section in a stable or barn where an animal is kept

THE LIFE OF A HORSE IN VICTORIAN TIMES

Black Beauty takes place in the mid-1800s, at a time when people used horses for transportation. Cars were not yet invented, and roads were often rough dirt trails. The nicest roads were made of stones.

Horses wore **horseshoes** to protect their hooves. They usually wore a **saddle** on their backs and headgear called a **bridle**. The bridle has a **bit** that goes into the horse's mouth, and it is attached to the **reins**. The rider pulls on the reins to give signals to the horse. In the story, Black Beauty had to wear a **checkrein**. This is a short rein that keeps the horse's head high. Black Beauty also wore leather flaps called **blinders** on his bridle. They shielded his eyes, making him look straight ahead.

There are different titles for people who handle horses. The **groom** takes care of the horse in its stable. For fine carriages, which hold a few people, a **coachman** steers the horses. For a quick, short ride, people might ride in a cab. This is a small and less fancy carriage driven by a **cabbie**.

Discussion Questions

1. Black Beauty's mother, Duchess, taught her son good manners. What are some good manners that you should use every day?

2. When he saw a dead horse in a cart, Black Beauty said he hoped that it was Ginger. Why did Black Beauty want Ginger to die?

3. Why did Lady York want Ginger and Black Beauty to wear the checkrein? Do you think that she treated the animals kindly?

4. At the end of the story, Black Beauty is called by his old name. Why does this make him feel happy?

WRITING PROMPTS

1. Toward the end of the story, Black Beauty thinks about Merrylegs and Ginger, his best friends. Describe each of the horses. What did they look like? How did they act?

2. Which place in the story do you think was Black Beauty's favorite? Describe your own favorite place and explain why it is your favorite.

3. Write a story about an animal in your life. What does the animal like? What does it dislike? What makes it sad or afraid? What makes it happy?

OTHER BOOKS

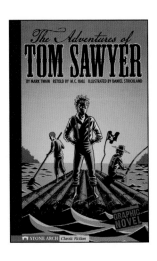

THE ADVENTURES OF TOM SAWYER

Tom Sawyer is the cleverest of characters, constantly outwitting those around him. Then there is Huckleberry Finn, the envy of the town's schoolchildren because he has the rare gift of complete freedom, never attending school or answering to anyone but himself. After Tom and Huck witness a murder, they find themselves on a series of adventures that lead them to some seriously frightening situations.

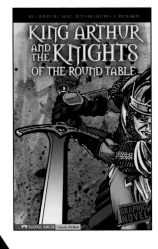

KING ARTHUR AND THE KNIGHTS OF THE ROUND TABLE

In a world of wizards, giants, and dragons, King Arthur and the Knights of the Round Table are the kingdom of Camelot's only defense against the threatening forces of evil. Fighting battles and saving those in need, the Knights of the Round Table can defeat every enemy but one — themselves!

ROBIN HOOD

Robin Hood and his Merrie
Men are the heroes of Sherwood
Forest. Taking from the rich and
giving to the poor, Robin Hood
and his loyal followers fight for
the downtrodden and oppressed.
As they outwit the cruel Sheriff
of Nottingham, Robin Hood and
his Merrie Men are led on a
series of exciting adventures.

TREASURE ISLAND

Jim Hawkins had no idea what
he was getting into when the
pirate Billy Bones showed up at
the doorstep of his mother's inn.
When Billy dies suddenly, Jim is left
to unlock his old sea chest, which
reveals money, a journal, and a
treasure map. Joined by a band of
honorable men, Jim sets sail on a
dangerous voyage to locate the loot
on a faraway island. The violent
sea is only one of the dangers they
face. They soon encounter a band
of bloodthirsty pirates determined
to make the treasure their own!

DATE DUE

OCT 2 2 2008			
JAN 3 0			
JAN 0 5			
DEC 1 4 2010			